LOST CITY OF THE DAMNED

by

I0665123

CHARLES NUETZEL

WRITING AS "ALEC RIVERE"

The Borgo Press
An Imprint of Wildside Press

MMVII

SECOND EDITION

CONTENTS

INTRODUCTION

Lost City of the Damned was my first adventure novel. I have always had a soft spot for it. It was written as the result of an editor asking for an original book to publish, which I didn't have at the time. So I rushed to my trusty typewriter, desperately searching my mind for an inspiration. And then I remembered my love for the books of writers like H. Rider Haggard and Edgar Rice Burroughs. Well, now, thought I, those stories were really fun. Maybe it would be a thrill and a half to write something along those lines.

I could offer up a lost-city adventure set in the deep jungles of some mysterious location. The idea instantly captivated me. I simply had to try one of those thrill-packed romantic adventures! I could take the reader into the very depths of the South American continent to watch two desperately struggling teams compete against one another in search of ancient treasure. Not a starkly original concept, but what the heck!

I was instantly hooked, as excited as a writer can get, and I frantically started whacking at the typewriter keyboard (remember, this was back in the 1960s!):

The valley waited, like it had been waiting for thousands of years—in silence and mystery—awaiting the touch of modern man.

It was a small valley, aged and savage, rugged and virgin except for the crumbled ruins at one of its further ends, under the lonely high snow-capped mountain. One large-peaked building was surrounded at every turn with rubble that may have once been a great city. Now it was waiting, like a magnificent monument of a dead age.

Nobody knew its origins; only legend and myths hung around it like some invisible mist clouding the long lost details of its wonder and glory.

The legend claimed that anyone who entered the sacred temple would die a horrible death.

Murder, danger, suspense haunt their trail as they search to discover the remains of an ancient civilization that may even have predated such legendary places as Mu and Atlantis. The promise of riches beyond imagination drove them to face unimaginable dangers in the lost city of the damned.

That would get even me to read the book! I hope you'll enjoy this literary excursion into the past, written near the beginning of my writing career.

—Charles Nuetzel
Thousand Oaks, California
July 2006

CHAPTER ONE

David Sheldon hadn't been to the island for over six years, not since his wife had died. The only reason he was returning now was because of a letter sent by Ed Norton, his one-time partner on a treasure hunt which had led the two men across the face of the world and ended with his wife's death. The contents of the letter was exciting enough to bring him half-way across the Pacific Ocean, even to the spot where he had lost the only thing he had ever loved, outside of money. It read:

Dear Dave,

First thing, you'll probably wonder why I'm writing you at this time—after such a long silence. But something of great importance has come to my attention and without your help it will be impossible to follow up on one of the greatest leads in history. Believe me when I say that I've really hit pay dirt.
Remember the Henderson expedition into Africa about fifteen years ago? They all had disappeared; were lost. As it turned out all are now dead, except for one. This one I've come

across and the story he has to tell is unbelievable! But that's not the important thing. It's what he brought back with him. I can't go into details right here, for several reasons. One is space and time. The other is that I don't want to take the chance of this information getting into the wrong hands.

Just take my word for it. If you want to get in on one of the biggest stories and adventures you have ever experienced—let alone a fortune that will make both of us rich for the rest of our lives, contact me at the WINTERS HOTEL on Telbrook Island.

Yours,

Ed Norton

It had been enough. Mention of the Henderson expedition was enough in itself. The complete confidence of Norton's words was more than enough to prove to Sheldon that there was more than just a lot of hot tropical air surrounding the South Sea Islands. One thing he knew was that Norton never said anything that wasn't true. If the man claimed that there was treasure or that there was a fortune— then that was exactly what there was. So it only took a few hours to telegram his friend and then make arrangements for a quick flight to the nearest airport and then connections for a charter boat to Telbrook Island.

Dave expected to find his friend at the dock,

waiting for him, or at least somebody to meet him.

There was nobody.

The island looked the same as it had seven years earlier: huge tall palms, white sandy shores, the one main street town, with the small theater bar, and WINTERS HOTEL. And the hot sun. Always the hot sun. Seemed like the heat followed him wherever he went.

Dave fanned himself with his pith helmet and looked across the score or so of faces that were moving along the dock. Nobody looked familiar. It was, at first, as if walking onto a strange and alien shore, as far as seeing anybody he knew. Then, suddenly, across the small land dock, he saw a dirty white cap hiding a bearded dark face.

A jolt of recognition charged through his body and he quickly started moving in the direction of the only familiar face he had yet seen.

"Charlie!" he cried, stepping up to the small thin man.

The other guy turned and looked up. For a moment his features seemed to be frozen with non-recognition and then they spread wide in surprise.

"Davy-boy, long time! Where've you been? What brings you around...I thought after..." the man's high squeaky voice faded out for a moment and then picked up again. "Gee, it's damn good to see you again."

They both grasped hands anxiously. "Ed Norton wrote me about something interesting—so here I am."

"Eddy-boy? I didn't even know he was around. And I *should* know!" Charlie Quinn exclaimed, an odd light crossing his eyes. "You know me. In on everything in the islands. Nothin' happens that Charlie don't know about."

For a moment Dave looked at the smaller thin man. "You leveling with me, Charlie?"

"What you take me for? A fool? Ain't heard nothing about Eddy-boy for some months."

Dave searched his pants pocket. Then he pulled out a letter and the telegram.

"Then explain this!" he demanded, extending them to the other man.

Charlie opened and read each line, slowly, in turn. Then his head shook from side to side and his finger tapped the edge of the telegram.

"Don't make sense. Maybe I'm cocked, but I ain't heard nothing about him being 'round."

They stood looking at each other for a long time and then Dave took the papers from Charlie's fingers and said: "How about coming along with me? We can talk it up a bit—and if Eddy's around, he'll be glad to see you, too."

"Okay—nothin' doin' today anyway...just been doin' the usual—loafin' a bit!"

They both started walking toward the Winters Hotel. It was the only rooming place on the island and not much of a hotel. The huge two-story house had once been the plantation home of a colonial governor who had settled on the island upon retirement some hundred years before. Since then, it had been remodeled as best it could be, without actually rebuilding it, to make the place into a rooming house. A small dining room and little bar were set up where the living room once had been. It was also the place where Dave's wife had been killed.

He tried to push all thoughts of her out of his

mind.

It didn't take long to get the room he had reserved from Los Angeles before taking off for his destination. Once inside the privacy of his small one room sleeping quarters he turned toward Charlie Quinn, looking savagely at the other man.

"Come on, you aren't playing games. You forget that I knew you when it counted. You never wasted time or money or effort for no reason."

Charles grinned, his thin lips opening across the large yellow stained uneven teeth. "Never could put much over on you, could I, Davy-boy?"

"Now tell me—where's Norton?"

"Dead!"

That was a shock that took several minutes for Dave to figure out. He couldn't believe the words, at first. Then slowly their meaning began to sink in.

"What the hell do you mean?"

"Just last night. Stabbed in the back. Nobody knows about it, yet, except me. I didn't want to let on that I knew anything about him, or the arrangements that were made...you see this is hot, plenty hot, believe me!"

Dave sat back on his small bed, still stunned by the startling news. He'd traveled halfway across the Pacific Ocean just to discover that the man he had come to see had been killed the night before. It didn't seem real. Even if they hadn't seen one another for years.

"How'd it happen?" he managed, wishing a drink was within reach.

Charlie shook his head from side to side. "Don't know. I went to his room this morning by the back way, so that nobody would see me—knocked on his door, and when he didn't answer, opened it with the skeleton key I carry around for this kind of work—he was lying face down on the floor. I didn't stop longer than it took to make sure he was dead—then I got the hell out of there."

Neither of them said anything for a long while; they just looked at each other blankly. Then finally, Dave searched his pockets for a cigarette. After finding the pack he offered Charlie one. Both lighted their own.

The death of Ed Norton didn't really mean anything personal to him—they had only been friends in a roundabout way. Mainly business interests had kept them together and in contact with each other. Though, of course, the death of anybody was a nasty business—especially murder! And especially if you knew the dead person. But the only emotion he felt was an edge of sorrow and a light fluttering of irritation in his stomach.

"Okay—what do you know about the deal?" Dave inquired. "What he wrote me about. What brought me here."

"Enough to make it interesting. Assuming, of course, you're interested!" The man offered a grin, and there was a bright twinkle in his eyes.

"Depends, I suppose. Tell me what I should be interested in!"

"How about five to ten million dollars? Is that interesting…enough?"

Dave jolted upright. He had expected maybe half a million at most, for both himself and Norton. Now it really looked like his ex-partner had hit upon something *big!* Real pay dirt. Not to be too unexpected, because the man had been hard core business, and never got excited about much of anything other than big bucks. Still, these kinds of numbers were beyond Dave's normal expectations. That kind of money would set a person up for life! Period!

"What do we need to do? Gotta rob the Bank of England?" he asked, studying the other man very critically.

"Not as simple as that—really."

"Not as simple?" he laughed.

"Has to do with a statue, made of solid gold, diamond, rubies, emeralds...just about every stone and rock you might imagine is on it. Norton was actually brimming over with excitement. Took his word for its value! I didn't see the real thing, of course, only seen the photo. And believe me it's really something. It knocked my eyeballs out—right out of their sockets. This is big! The only thing is..."

"The catch?"

"The catch! And believe me—it's something. But even then...catch or not, it is a huge pay-off!"

"And, tell me more..." He was now totally intrigued.

"Well, to begin with—"

Just then there was a knock on the door.

They looked at each other. Then Dave got up and walked over to the door and opened it. There was a beautiful blonde woman standing there, looking as innocent as all heaven, except for the shiny black revolver held in her white gloved hands, pointed at Dave's stomach.

His first reaction was shock, and then as he saw the all but perfect features of her face and the flowing full figure veiled by her light summer dress, he

13

had another reaction—*desire.* This was a woman who could seduce a dead elephant! There was something classy about her slim, yet well shaped body. His eyes lingered for a moment on that lovely image, a bit intrigued and most of all somewhat stunned.

Then he remembered the gun again and took a step backwards. All this took only a split moment, just one lingering sweep of his eyes along her body and then back to the gun.

"What's the meaning of—?"

"Quiet! We don't have time to waste. We gotta get out of here—fast!" she announced in tight low words. Her voice matched the lovely vision, both serious, but low and inviting.

She pointed the gun at Charlie Quinn. "You, too. Both of you come along." She hid the gun under her large white purse. "Don't make the mistake of thinking you can jump me because I'm a woman."

"Don't worry. I don't argue with a gun!" Dave said, keeping a safe distance between himself and the woman. Take the gun away and he'd want to swiftly narrow that distance! In fact he was feeling a bit light headed just looking at her—and it wasn't fear that raced his heart a beat faster.

"Walk down the hall toward the back entrance. There's a car awaiting for you there."

The two of them carefully did as she told them, taking no chance of making her think they would be trying anything other than what they were told.

It wasn't that Dave Sheldon was a coward. Only a matter mathematics. If someone had a gun on him, no matter who it might be, even such a knockout of

14

a man killer as this woman, he doesn't mess around. He was crafty enough to figure that it was just as easy for a girl as a man to kill somebody if she had a gun in her hand. Just squeeze the trigger. And no matter how invitingly attractive and seductive the outer package, the inner personality might be quite twisted—and deadly.

There was a car waiting for them outside the hotel with a local in the driver's seat.

"Get in," she told them.

Once they were seated and the door slammed shut behind them, she moved to the front seat and turned in their direction, leveling the gun so that neither of them would get away with any funny business. "I'm sorry to have to get you two in such a dramatic way…"

"Just exactly what do you think you are doing'?" Dave demanded, feeling a bit less threatened. "What do you want with us?"

"Yeah, Miss. We don't know you none—how you know you got the right men?" Charlie put in quickly.

"Why, you're Charlie Quinn, island bum and beachcomber—and this other man is David Sheldon, one time adventurer." She smiled prettily, her even white teeth showing beautifully in the hot sun. "Does that make you more welcomed?"

"Christ!" Charlie exploded.

"Okay, then…" Dave started to say.

She broke him off with a wave of the gun. "Not right now, Mister Sheldon. You'll just have to wait."

The words had been soft spoken but were demanding. The two men lapsed into silence.

CHAPTER TWO

Fifteen minutes later they found themselves driving along a narrow jungle mud road, heading south across the island.

"Where are you taking us?" Dave asked.

"You'll find out soon enough," was all she offered, though her voice was softer, just a little more relaxed and friendly.

It was only a few more minutes before they came to an abrupt clearing in the tangled green jungle.

There was a large bungalow-style house before them. The car came to a stop in front of it and then the girl slid out of her seat, opened the car door and ordered them out.

They were directed up the few steps to the large porch and into the back of the house.

Dave found himself in a huge living room, furnished with old-fashioned furniture, bookcases filled with books and the walls lined with weapons of all kinds.

The woman stayed with them but the driver went into the back of the house.

"Make yourselves at home," she suggested, indicating the large leather chairs in the middle of the room, near the open fireplace. "It'll only be a moment."

Her attitude, now that they had arrived at the house, had changed slightly. It seemed friendlier, not as hard or demanding.

Dave was just seating himself when a tall, white-haired man walked into the room. For a moment he couldn't be sure if he were seeing right. He blinked his eyes several times, looking carefully at the well-known face he recognized from photographs and newsreels.

"No—it can't be!" he blurted out. *"Doctor Henderson!"*

Dave Sheldon finally came out of his daze. "I thought that you were dead."

"No—I was the only one who survived to return to civilization." The tall older man walked across the room toward a small cabinet. Opening the small doors he displayed a liquor supply that seemed to cover anything a person might wish or desire. "Will you two join me in a drink?"

Dave's mind was beginning to work fast, covering the events of the last hour, since he'd arrived on the island. First, Charlie acts like he doesn't know about Norton being on the island, and then in the privacy of Sheldon's room tells the truth about the man's death. The girl shows up with a gun and forces them to come to this place.

And now Henderson shows up almost from the grave, stunning all of them. The news media had reported him lost.

Henderson—the only one who survived the expedition. And in the letter he had received it had said that only one person had survived...then Henderson must be on his side... He shook his head. *It didn't figure!*

18

"You want a drink, Mr. Sheldon?" Henderson repeated for the third time.

"Yes...I could use one." Dave stood and started walking in a half circle. "I don't get this."

"You will, believe me, my friend," Henderson told Dave, handing him a drink. "I'm sorry for Jean's rather dramatic way of getting you here, but there were several good reasons for the method. One being no wiggle room. Time is running a tight noose around our actions. What happened to our mutual friend last night...well that is serious cause for alarm and...quite frankly, we have to be very, very careful!"

Henderson walked across the room to one of the leather easy chairs and sat tiredly down. "A hot day...a very hot day it is."

There was an awkward silence while nobody seemed to know what to say or do. Dave took the time to look over Jean, this time with a more careful eye. And without the threatening gun between them. It made quite a difference!

She had a figure that would knock the eyeballs out of any man's head. The way the front of her dress pushed outwards was an eye catcher. His eyes followed the length of her curving body. It pinched in at the waist and flared at the hips. What he could see of her legs, below her skirt, was enough to make him feel sure that she had a very beautiful pair.

She suddenly glanced in his direction. There was a half-friendly smile in her eyes. Then she looked away. In that moment there was a sense of silent communication; but what it said was uncertain, vague, guarded.

Charlie coughed and finally Henderson looked

19

up, took a swallow of his drink and then said: "I imagine you wonder why you were brought here."

Dave turned and looked at the older man. He stared at him for a moment and then tried to make his voice sound light and airy as he said: "Well, you know, Doctor, I'm not usually brought around to strangers' houses at gunpoint!"

That chilled the otherwise heated room.

Henderson took a swallow of his drink. "There's a long story involved—and good reasons for what I've done...the way I brought you here." He leaned back in his chair and looked at empty space. "Let me tell you something about...about what has happened to me since I escaped from Africa some five years ago.

"Escaped?" Dave asked, startled, and not knowing quite why.

"I'll have to give it to you fast, since time is the most important thing...and we have so little of it. As you must know, the expedition went into Africa for the usual things. A hot lead to a hidden city. We didn't know what culture, or even what era it was from, only that something existed.

"Usually, nowadays, Africa is considered not quite so 'dark' as it once was. Everything is quite civilized—but there are still places that are little known. Few, that's for sure!

"Anyway, we found what we were after. Only thing was that it turned out to be more than just a ruined old crumbling hidden city. The fact of the matter was that it turned out to be a quite live culture. Savage—and living in a very primitive condition—but that wasn't the main point. It was the remains of the temple that held my interest, and every

20

other person's interest in the expedition. You see—everything in it was made of solid gold with jewels of every kind.

"The only thing was that the natives guard this treasure as if it were worth more than just all the money in the world. They claim it is taboo—that some kind of curse is attached to it. They won't go near it and won't let anybody else near it."

"But I heard," broke in Dave, "that you'd gotten some kind of...Charlie here saw a picture of a golden statue—"

"Right. And just that picture alone cost the lives of several men. Each died a violent and horrible death at the hands of the natives. It would seem that what the so-called curse doesn't do, they make sure happens—at least in the surrounding valley where they live."

"What's to keep us from going into the place in big numbers with a lot of fire power—?"

This time it was Jean who spoke up. *"Nothing except the curse!"*

Everybody turned in her direction, surprised and shocked by the sudden outburst.

Dave found it hard to keep a smile from crossing his features. "Certainly, you don't believe in such hocus pocus nonsense as curses, do you?"

"This one...is different!" she announced, a bit tensely.

"Well. Okay. Then tell me: what exactly is the curse?"

"That anybody who touches the statue will die a horrible and terrible death."

"Well—Doctor Henderson isn't dead."

"And he never touched the statue!"

"So?"

Henderson now offered: "So everybody who did ended up dead—*dying violently.* So we were careful...not to touch the statue!"

"You have the statue?" Charlie cried excitedly.

"We had it."

"What...what happened to it?" Dave asked breathlessly.

"It's in Africa."

"Where?"

"That's just it—we aren't exactly sure where. But never mind that."

There was a heavy silence, thick with tension. Then Henderson continued. "You see, there were quite a few of us on the expedition. It took months to find the city and then months to find a way into the tomb without the natives bothering us. Only trouble came when they discovered our nighttime diggings—and that's when things got a little out of hand. We tried to explain that we were a scientific expedition in sign language and a few of the words we'd picked up of their speech—but it was useless. They believed themselves the guardians of this holy place and wouldn't let anybody inside—*not even themselves.* They were afraid of some ancient gods. But believe me—all this argument was of no value—none at all.

"You see, in order to escape with our lives we had to actually end up fighting our way out. We had been caught inside the temple—and we had just decided to leave it, for their sake. Trapped, so to speak—in the fight that followed, something happened...nobody knew exactly what. Maybe it was the sound of our gunfire—the vibrations—but

22

something clicked off inside the temple some-where...and the very walls themselves started to fall apart.

"We got out just in time—one thing we had learned—but that comes later, though. Somehow we managed to get away from the valley—what was left of us—only three of the original members and one golden statue. The trip back to civilization killed off the other two men who had been weak-ened by wounds and almost finished me off."

"But the statue?" Charlie questioned eagerly.

"I don't know. It was with me—wrapped up in cloth. And in a box."

"So that he couldn't touch it!" Jean said in a voice that said, *I told you so.*

"Well anyway I became a little—well, out of my head—and the next thing I knew I was in some mis-sionary's home—in bed. I'd been there for over a week. They told me that the only thing I had with me was what I'd carried on my back. One item was a camera with a roll of exposed film in it."

"So where does that leave us?" Dave wanted to know; feeling a slight inner irritation for having been brought half across an ocean to hear an in-credible story that led to nothing.

"Just there!" Henderson exclaimed dramatically, stepping up to a large globe of the world in the cor-ner of the room. He was pointing to South America. "That's where it leads us. To another city. And an-other fortune."

Dave felt like exploding in all directions at once. He had spent a goodly sum of money just to hear all *this nonsense!*

"I see you aren't convinced," Henderson commented. "Let me explain. In the temple there were huge designs and markings on the walls. And one large map. Incredible as it might seem, it was a map of the world...And on it were indicated several cities—across the whole face of the globe. *Yet, this temple and all that was in it had apparently been built several thousand years before the birth of Christ."*

There was a stunned silence as Dave and Charlie Quinn took in what had been said.

"So you see—that's the reason for all the careful secrecy and bringing you here at 'gun-point'. We don't want anybody to know about anything. Already there are too many people knowing about our plans. As a result Ed Norton is dead. I liked him, trusted him and he valued you...that's why you're here, now."

"But—but how do you expect to find this lost city—and how do you know it is still there or still has any treasures in it...?"

"First: I took a detailed picture of the map. Second: I've spent several years studying the different locations—both for clues of civilizations and for signs of geological shifts and changes in the lands. There is still one city—apparently quite important in its time—that must be in some state of ruins, perhaps, but existing. If we can find this city, it will not only bring riches to all of us, of course—but also be of great historical and scientific value. You see—it may clear up, once and for all, the mystery of that legend of Atlantis...or the myth of Mu! Even more, perhaps. There was one word that kept cropping up now and then: Haldton...or Halodolen. Translations are difficult to deal with, to be truthful. But there

24

were other ancient hints in several old documents that I've come across that offered a strange reference to a land in the Pacific Ocean, of some amazingly advanced civilization that may have existed even previous to all other legendary places like Mu or Atlantis."

"Atlantis?" Charlie Quinn questioned. "I know that ... place. Ain't it fiction?"

"Nobody really knows. A lot of theories," Henderson offered with a shrug.

Dave asked: "Mu? Weren't there a bunch of books published in the 1800s about Mu?"

"Yes. I see you're somewhat informed."

"Not really. Read them as a kid. Seemed like fiction to me."

"Perhaps. Published during the same time frame many strange changes were taking place in the world—religious movements forming...well never mind all that. Some considered the author a bit of a fake! But he did offer some interesting ideas concerning evidence of ancient civilizations, one of which may have existed in the Pacific Ocean area, way back when."

"I remember something about a lost continent disappearing under the ocean," Dave offered, grinning uneasily.

"Well, we really don't know much about all that, now, do we? A lot of things that the scientific world just doesn't know about...yet. That's what drives us on. But...the numbers I was coming across in these texts...are, quite frankly, downright impossible. I mean, the supposed age of such a mythological land. Like 20,000 BC. Or maybe, even, 40,000 BC. And that would be at the very dawn of

25

modern man…well, never mind that. Once I came across a line which, loosely translates: *He was a warrior named Thoris from the watery lands of Haldow-lo-an.* Something like that."

Jean laughed lightly. "Haldolen! That's how I'd pronounce it. I like that better. But that's all fanciful! You can't believe all those ancient texts, Dad!"

"I don't!" the scientist admitted. "But it sure takes one down an interesting mind-game."

Dave was glancing at the two, suddenly startled to discover that the woman and scientist were related. He had thought her, perhaps, his secretary or young girl friend.

Jean shrugged with a wide grin. "Dad loves exploring all these imaginative ideas. Sorta fun, I have to admit."

"And," her father stated, "Not very scientific…just a hobby that keeps my mind lucid and flexible enough to entertain what would otherwise seem rather wildly fantastic possibilities."

Dave was too intrigued by Jean, now, that he knew more about the woman. He watched her as she continued in a liltingly pleasant voice:

"A game that is really silly stuff. Can you imagine a warrior from 20,000 BC…well okay, why not make it Thoris from 30,000 BC?" She laughed again. "Dad enjoys imagining all kinds of things like that. In his off hours."

They all laughed a bit; then, in a very serious voice, Henderson said: "Well, never mind all that. We're talking, realistically, about Mu, perhaps, or whatever it was actually called by its inhabitants. Or, maybe, something else. But hard reality! Whatever it is, we're working with something that exists here and now! Believe me. I *know*!"

He paused for a moment, then added: "Now tell me, Mr. Sheldon. *Are you interested?*"

LOST CITY OF THE DAMNED, BY CHARLES NUETZEL

CHAPTER THREE

Ruby Turner sat there in the yacht's small cabin, feeling uneasy and, at the same time, excited. The expedition was on its way and she was feeling pretty good. There were three European partners, and a crew of five men. A small but compact group that could be controlled.

She was waiting for Vern to join her, feeling slightly uneasy and a bit squirmy. She needed him.

It was a hot night, a tropic night, just like two nights before when she'd been with that slob, Norton. Even if her tastes in men were pretty liberal and even if she liked sex—a lot—she hadn't enjoyed what happened between Norton and herself. She'd approached Norton at the hotel bar, brazenly flirting. She had let the man "convince" her to join him in a private party. He proved to be a very fast mover. And obviously drunk.

His room was hot with the heavy tropic burn only possible in the South Seas. It was also heated by the desperate aggressive fury of the man coming at her so violently the moment the door was closed. With the right man, such aggression would have been quite exciting. But she had no desire, at all, for this seedy little bastard.

"Don't!" she said, pushing him very gently back. "Please stop!"

"Come on, get off it, bitch!" the man growled. The man's breathing was heavy and his breath acid and revolting.

"Wait!" Ruby now made her move, reaching for her purse.

"What the hell for?" he demanded, his hand on her breast.

"Just this, honey," she managed to murmur in her most seductive voice, surging up against his pawing fingers.

That distracted him, just long enough.

Without warning she moved with lightning speed. Her hand came out of her purse and without even a pause thrust furiously at him. The man gave out a scream of pain, his huge arms flinging upwards, his back arching. Then he fell forward, face smashing to the floor. There was a large, bloody knife sticking in his chest.

The woman stood. The moonlight, which floated through the open window, highlighted her delicate, pretty features. The full sensual lips moved in a crooked smile as she looked down at the dead man.

Leaning over, she slowly pulled the knife from his back. Wiping it clean on his shirt.

"So much for you, Mr. Treasure hunter!" she said coldly. "Really too bad you weren't...somebody I'd have enjoyed!"

She smiled for a moment, considering the growing need she felt. Ruby liked men—a lot! Some called her oversexed, a nymph. Slut. Tramp. She didn't really mind all that. Whatever they wanted to call her, just so they were a turn-on in bed. But even she could be picky. And Norton was a turn-off.

So much for him, she decided, pleased at her work.

Quickly she placed the knife in her purse, walked to the dirty mirror that hung over the sink, and made her face up. Then she turned and started searching the room. The dresser, and then under the mattress and bed and then lastly in the clothes closet. Finally she found what she was looking for. A small envelope with several photos in it.

Taking a deep sigh of relief, she walked out of the room, without even taking a second look at the dead body of the man on the floor.

Norton was a pig. Not like her man. Vern Yates was something different.

Now they were several miles north of Telbrook Island in a small yacht, slowly making its way towards its destination in South America.

She felt uneasy about appearing to be a minor player in this adventure—but it really didn't matter, as long as things turned out right.

If Vern Yates wanted to play Big Man, Big Boss, it was okay with her. The other two men would be kept under control and that left her with Vern to keep her needs satisfied. Just as he'd done yesterday when she'd brought the things taken from Norton to her man.

She hadn't waste any time in making her needs obvious. She moved into his arms the moment they were alone. When he ran his hands along the curve of her breast she melted against him. He pulled down the strap of her dress and unclasped the bra, and from the trembling action of his fingers she was sure that he was about to rip the dress the rest of the way off her body.

31

"Oh, Vern," she murmured in his ear, working the lobe between her teeth and large sensual lips. "You're the best"

"And you deserve the best—after what you did..." His breathing was heavy with excitement as he moved his face downwards along her shoulder, toward the pink tipped mound of flesh which was aching and longing for him.

A moan ran through her body a moment later. She felt his hand reaching down, sliding toward the long tapering legs.

She arched upwards against him as she felt his fingers searching along the elastic band of her panties. After a moment they had been ripped off and she felt him surge down hard against her. The next moments were wild, unrelenting madness as their two bodies beat out a furious rhythm. She felt as if her body was being thrust into a sea of ecstatic bliss, a storm that ravished every nerve.

Then suddenly it was over and he was lying beside her on the bed, breathing hard and for a long moment finding it difficult to do anything but try to catch his breath.

After a long time the man sat up. "You're something wild, baby!"

"I needed you...after what happened last night! That Norton bastard tried to rape me!" she cursed, starting to dress.

He laughed. "I thought you liked it rough!"

"You know it—but only with a man I want...like you!" She laughed in delight. "Sometimes I think you could do anything to me! And I'd..."

She shrugged that off.

His eyes were feasting on her breasts, as they slowly disappeared behind the cloth. "Face it Ruby...you like it with any man!"

A hurt expression crossed her face, but she couldn't completely deny his statement.

"But not with a damn bastard like him!" she snapped.

"Well, what the hell? He's dead. We got the photos. Nothing else really counts! The dumb fool blabbed too much!"

"Well, that's to our advantage, Vern," she pouted, teasingly, sliding down next to him, and caressing his cheek with her hand. "You and me mean something—don't we?"

"Sure. Sure!" His voice sounded bored and tired. "I wonder what's keeping Carver and Johnston? They should have been here before now." He stood and started dressing. "We don't have all the time in the world."

"Honey—you forget they don't know about the change of plans!"

"Hell—that don't matter." He turned, now fully dressed and looked at Ruby. "Yeah, I guess it does matter. You had to do a lot to make those changes. Now we have a chance of getting that big money before Henderson—otherwise we would have had to try joining them..."

There was a knock on the door.

"Who is it?" Vera asked, wiping sweat from his thick dark features.

"Carver...and Johnston," a voice called back.

He reached for the door and let the two men in, and then closed it again. "About time you got here!"

The tall European-dressed Johnston looked appraisingly at Ruby, his eyes moving along her sensual figure, which the dress did nothing to hide.

"I see you had something to keep you entertained," the man smiled, still looking at the woman.

"That's my business, Mister Johnston!" Vern snapped angrily.

"Okay, okay!"

"Let's stop the quibbling," Captain Carver suggested, finding it hard to keep his eyes off Ruby. She was a woman that few men could ignore.

"Okay," Vern said, his voice becoming all business. "There's a change of plans."

"What now?" sighed Johnston.

"Take it easy. Believe me, with the money you are investing in this..."

"The last bit of cash I could get together."

"It's enough—believe me. The deal was that I'd get us to the lost city...and you'd put up the cash to back the expedition. Okay then—I got the road map to the city!"

Carver and Johnston let out a surprised gasp. It was more than either could have dreamed possible.

"When do we leave?" Johnston finally asked.

"Tonight. The sooner the better. We have to get there before the Henderson group does. Set up a few booby traps along the way—and one by one rid ourselves of the competition. Then money enough for all of us to live the rest of our lives without another worry!" Vern's eyes were large and gleaming, his lips curled back in an ugly but eager grin. "Yes, more money than we'll ever know what to do with!"

Ruby lay there in the bunk, fighting the inner annoyance at being put in the background; especially after what she'd been responsible for. But

Ruby knew that the best way to control men was to let them control her. By playing the backfield she ran the game in the long run. Yet, for the present, she resented the role. The men were in the other room, making their nasty little plans. She'd give them a few minutes, then join them.

* * * * * * *

Vern Yates felt satisfied with how things were working out. Ruby was a neat partner to have around, both in bed and out. She'd managed a lot, so far. Just so she kept in her place. He didn't like the idea of being run by a female. Not Vern Yates. And the woman let him be top dog—and that's what counted.

As long as Carter and Johnston accepted his leadership things would run smoothly. They had one thing in common: a driving desire for riches.

The two other bearded whites were sitting in the small captain's cabin with Vern. There was a chessboard set up between them on a short desk. A fifth of vodka was open and half full. One man wore a battered captain's hat; another was dressed in neat European summer clothes.

Vern Yates, was sitting there, very carefully watching the other two.

The neatly dressed one had the look of soft education and easy life; the Captain looked hard and bitter, his beady eyes red-rimmed and greed-filled. The two were slightly drunk, as was Vern, but deadly serious. Neither was paying much attention to the game; there were other matters far more important and serious to keep their minds *working*.

Carver had brought the story about Norton to Vern's attention and was dominating the conversation.

"The plan—you see," the Captain was saying, "is not to let the Henderson group know anything about us...that has worked out pretty well. Just have to keep in the background and then when things are working out right—that's soon enough to jump them."

"Look, Carver, I don't want to get into anything that might...well, be..."

"Mister Johnston—you were told in England that there were dangers—you invested in the project..."

Vern interrupted. "You ain't backing out now!"

"That's not it. Just that I want to make sure that we are careful! I'm not interested in getting in trouble with the law, you know."

"We've been plenty careful. Ruby was the one who took all the risks. It's just good that she's one hell of a sexy bitch!" Vern continued, leaning forward. "And one sexy little killer!"

"But what do we do to the Henderson group?" Johnston wanted to know, "I mean—they'll have to be..."

"Killed!" Carver grinned.

Johnston looked from one to the other.

"Why not?" Vern questioned.

Johnston shrugged his shoulders. "I don't give a damn —just as long as we get away with it."

"Why can't we? And it'll be worth any risk—a fortune that will keep us living high for the rest of our lives!" Vern Yates told them, laughing and taking a long swallow of his drink. "A fortune—for the rest of our natural lives!"

Just then Ruby walked in.

"God it's hot," she moaned, leaning over the table and picking up the vodka bottle.

"I need this!" she announced, smiling at Johnston.

The Englishman smiled warmly back and his hand reached out and touched hers. "Any time, baby."

"Get the hell out of here!" Vern yelled, standing and jerking her away from the table and Johnston and the bottle of vodka. "Get back to your cabin—and now!"

She looked at him for a long moment her eyes narrowing and her lips trembling slightly. A red flush ran up her face, "Don't take forever..."

He laughed, knowingly, "I won't!"

Without another word she turned and walked out, slamming the door after her.

"You, my dear friend," Vern told Johnston, "Can keep your hands off her—the treasure's all of ours...but Ruby's *mine!*"

Johnston looked angrily at the other man, but didn't say anything.

"That goes for you, too, Carver!" Yates snapped, taking another swallow of his drink and then turning and walking from the room.

There wasn't any love lost between them, he thought, stepping into his and Ruby's quarters. *The only thing that holds them together is that treasure.*

He moved over to where Ruby was lying on her bunk. Without a word he grabbed the woman. She didn't struggle, she wouldn't dare. She didn't even want to.

Like two savage beasts, they devoured one another in a fit of mindless passion.

CHAPTER FOUR

Three weeks had whipped by so fast that David Sheldon found it hard to really keep track of what was happening.

Now they were off the coast of South America's Amazon River, on the brink of the greatest adventure ever experienced by him. On the search of a lost civilization, scientific secrets and a fortune which none of them could spend for the rest of their lives, if they gave money away as fast as they could. It was a good feeling to know that finally the world was almost open to him. He'd soaked everything he had into financing this expedition—and he knew that it would be worth it.

As he looked out over the edge of the large yacht's railing at the calm ocean, he heard a rustling behind him and turned.

It was Jean Henderson. That was a surprise. Up until then she seemed to be ignoring him. Now she was smiling. "Hello, what are you doing out here all alone?"

For a moment he didn't quite know what to say. The friendly air about her was so different from the last weeks. For some reason she had seemed half afraid of him.

"Just looking at the setting sun," he said in a soft smiling voice. "Join me?"

A slight wall of resistance went across her delicate features, but she came to the railing next to him.

"It's beautiful, isn't it?" she said pausing a bit in a hesitant tone.

He just nodded, taking in the delicately light scent of perfume that surrounded her. It was hard to ignore her shorts and tight-fitting blouse, partly opened at the top, but he managed averting his eyes by just looking out straight toward the distant shore of South America.

For a long time they both stood there, each silently aware of the other, but not looking at each other.

He wanted to reach for her, but knew that would be a fatal mistake. Ever since he'd first seen Jean Henderson, the Doctor's daughter, he had wanted to take her in his arms. But the days had been hectic. They were all preoccupied and focused on getting supplies—guns—setting up for a charter boat in Rio de Janeiro. Then they had to arrange their flight to the Brazilian Capitol City, locate this yacht for charter and plan further arrangements for the trip inland after they had gone as far as the yacht could take them. There had been times when the two of them had been thrown together, but she had remained cool and distant.

Now this.

"What are the others doing?" he asked, turning in her direction.

"Charlie's getting drunk—as usual. "

"That's the old boy—"

"He makes me nervous. I don't know if I can trust him."

"He's harmless."

"The way he...looks at me, gives me the shivers," she admitted.

"I'll talk to him. If you want."

"That'd be nice." She actually smiled up at him, then looked nervously away. As if desperate to change the topic, she said: "Dad's working on his maps—"

"I guess that's usual, too."

"Always." She smiled a little sadly. "A dedicated scientist and somewhat of a romantic...an interesting combination. He used to read science fiction to me when I was as little girl. Those Edgar Rice Burroughs books about lost cities and—well, anyway, he really is quite serious, regardless of all that other side of him."

"Guess it's quite a hard bit being a famous scientist's daughter," he commented conversationally.

She shrugged. "I did my research and study when he was in Africa. I got my degree back then. But...useful as it is, I'm not as dedicated as he is. I'm just simply curious and partially serious about ancient ruins...I mean, whatever we find should be turned over to the authorities. Yet, I'm just like you, interested in the money, too. They'll give us a big enough cut...doing it legally makes it possible to save the hard scientific evidence. Beyond that...well, I don't know."

She hesitated, then said, awkwardly, "I mean...I want more out of life than mere research and things like that."

"A home? Family?" he inquired.

"Probably. I suppose. In time." She was looking out across the water, into the night, but sounded quite nervous, uneasy.

"No man in mind?" he inquired.

She glance at him and for a moment looked as if she were about to say it wasn't any of his business, but instead she turned away, shrugged.

The silence was long, and he was painfully aware of her lovely form outlined against the night sky. He wanted to reach out and touch her.

"A little hot, isn't it?" he suddenly blurted out.

She turned; looking startled by his sudden statement, "I guess so."

Their eyes met, searchingly. It was the first time they had really given each other such a deep, penetrating stare.

Her eyes were deep blue, reflecting the color of the ocean surrounding them on all sides. She had a youthful, almost boyish look about her. That wasn't to say she was anything near mannish appearing. A total woman! But sporty—outdoors type. The way he had always liked them. The way his wife had been.

All of a sudden her mood seemed to change and she unexpectedly said in a low, husky voice:

"I've been wondering...I haven't figured you out. I mean...just what kind of a man *are* you? "

That was a question out of left field, and it was hard to know exactly what she meant by it. Was she actually being flirtatious?

"In what way?" he smiled, winking.

"Not *that* way!" she quickly snapped in a slightly nervous voice, as a deep red flush worked up her high cheeks.

The heated reaction was too fast, too quick. He couldn't help feeling sorry for her, though.

"I didn't exactly mean—well—" he offered,

42

shrugging. "It's just that the way you worded the question..."

"That isn't important anyway." She had recovered.

"Well, tell me something about yourself."

"What?"

"Anything." *Yes,* he realized, *anything at all would be wonderful!*

She had regained her composure and turned her eyes away from his to look out at the far horizon. The sun was almost below the edge of the world. It outlined her features with a light orange line; her delicate upswept nose; large eyes and full lips—ripe and soft; her small chin and smooth rounded jaw; the white cream of her throat and silk of her slender shoulders and arms. They were all painted in deep rich gold: red-gold.

"I just grew up like a lot of girls. I guess. Mom, before she died, raised me for the most part. After she was gone—I was just a kid then—I took care of Dad. He always needed caring for—you know how scientists are...and he's...well he took care of me, too. Taught me how to think. He's a wonderful person...really. Even if he's distant at times, lost in his own private mental world. I mean—so scientifically minded—No, that's not what I really mean. He's...well, Dad is clear-headed—knows where he's going—and he's watched out for me...when he's around and focused."

"Been gone a lot?"

"Yes, I suppose. Very busy."

"Lost in his world?" he managed, wondering what kind of childhood she really had, and what her relationship with Dr. Henderson was really all about.

"But he's been there for me...I mean in—well, you know—done the best he could."

"Without a wife around to take over the mother role?"

"I suppose. Very protective, at times. You surely must know how fathers are." She laughed nervously, as if she wasn't quite sure of what fathers were like; as if she was beginning to wonder about herself.

He reached out and gently caressed her shoulder. For a moment she half smiled then nervously looked away, stepping back out of reach. "Dad—well he was the one who taught me almost everything during my teens. And we've been mutually supportive. He's something of an absent-minded man about everyday things. Sometimes I think he'd be lost without me..."

"That's silly!"

She turned and looked, startled, at him. "How would you know?"

"It's just normal for a daughter to live her own life. Your father has his own world and life and career—you can't live it for him."

"That's not what I said!" Her voice was shaking slightly as if she were confused. "What I meant—I...mean..."

"I wish you understood..." She stiffened and looked away once more. "Why did I say that...why should I care what you...?"

He moved closer to her, a new understanding and tenderness shifting through his mind. Reaching out, he tried to pull her to him. But on contact she stepped hurriedly away, giving him a quick nervous look.

There was a long silence after that. Then she turned and smiled. "I'm sorry. That wasn't really nice of me..."

The way her eyes sparkled almost sadly and the way she seemed to be leaning half in his direction made the desire well up in him.

He couldn't help feeling sorry for her. She was confused and unsure of herself. She didn't seem to know the difference between passion and love or affection.

Tenderly, he reached for her, again and when she backed away half frightened, he stepped closer to her and pulled her firmly to him.

She didn't struggle at first, but instead her body seemed to be stiff and frozen to inactivity. Then the expression on her face showed bewilderment and fear and confusion, and for a moment she seemed to relax.

For only an instant did she remain in his arms and then without any warning she squirmed desperately and twisted from his grasp.

"Stop it!" she cried, swinging a stinging savage slap across his face.

Then she froze. Horror clouded her eyes. Her whole face became distorted with concern and fright.

"Oh, God—I'm sorry!" she murmured. For a moment she looked at him and then slowly started backing up. "I'm...sorry—I didn't mean..."

Abruptly she turned and ran down the deck. A moment later she disappeared into her cabin.

He was too stunned to do anything but stand there looking at the spot where she had disappeared.

His emotions and mind were working like a speeding and confused machine.

Hurt. From the slap. More pain from the way she had backed away from him, confused and crying.

But maybe that wasn't her fault. Maybe that was Henderson's fault: The scientist who teaches his daughter to respect nothing but the cold impersonal approach of the scientific mind.

Tell a girl, like Jean, something like that and it could easily cause confusion. She was warm, loveable, and affectionate—that much he felt sure of.

It would take time. That much he knew now. A lot of time and care and…

And what?

Not *love!* He didn't like that word. Not after his wife—he could never love again.

But that was silly—couldn't a person love twice?

No! his mind screamed, *no—he wasn't in love!*

Jean was just a woman—and that was all. Just one hell of an attractive woman whom he'd certainly like to ravish from head to foot!

CHAPTER FIVE

Johnston was lounging in his bunk, sipping a rum and coke when Ruby stepped in, a large rum bottle in her hands.

"Hi, there—" she cried brightly. "What're you doing all by yourself?"

He looked up, startled by the sudden interruption of his thoughts and slightly unnerved by the abrupt appearance of the very object of his dreams. All the men wanted a piece of her action.

"What are you doing here?" he demanded in a much harsher sounding voice than he had meant.

"Oh, want me to go?" she asked icily, her eyes narrowing and the bright smile leaving her sensual full lips.

"No—no!" he quickly assured her, sitting up and turning fully in her direction. For the first time he noticed the way she was dressed—or rather not dressed. She had on shorts and a bra.

What a classy little, voluptuous tramp the woman was, he thought in amusement. Not, necessarily, the type he came across in England.

She laughed, pleased, as she noticed the direction his eyes took along her lush figure, pausing at the large swells of her breasts.

"It's hot!" she announced, as if that explained her semi-nude condition. "And we're all adults here, on this...cruise!"

"Well—to what do I owe this rather unexpected visit?" he asked, standing and offering her a chair—the only one in the small cabin.

She shook her head and moved to the narrow bunk. "Nobody else around. They all went ashore on business."

"Of course—I forgot..."

They just looked at each other for a long time, not saying anything; but the way her eyes swept his hard, lean body left no question in his mind what she was thinking or desiring. Ruby was a very down-to-earth, basic woman. Only the fact that Yates claimed her as his own, personal property had kept Johnston at arm's distance. But right now, there was no question about what Ruby had in mind. She wasn't the coy type. And she was the only female around. One couldn't be choosy. And this lush lady certainly wasn't the type of female a man could easily ignore, nor turn down. The woman had been watching him all during the trip and the looks she tossed his way were downright flirtatious.

"I brought along a bottle. Thought we might celebrate a little!"

"Celebrate what?"

"Well—do we have to have something...don't be stuffy—" she laughed, her head moving backward, her chest thrusting outwards.

He couldn't keep his eyes away from voluptuous breasts flowing over the tight bra, straining as if wanting to burst free. He was already feeling his rum making him a bit light-headed.

She leaned forward again and then looked deeply at him. "If you really need something to

48

celebrate, consider that we're alone…at last! I think you've wanted that!"

He sat down beside her and quickly reached and pulled her to him. *What the hell,* he figured, *take what he could get!*

"Come on, big boy—not so *fast!*" she laughed, struggling only slightly. "Well, maybe…why not?"

Then their lips met for an excited instant and he felt hers parting under his and the searching eagerness of her tongue as it darted outwards seeking.

She pushed against him, her whole body working hard and heated against his.

"Oh I've wanted you!" she murmured in a low husky voice. "Right from the start."

"What stopped you?" he breathed against her shoulder, playing into her game. "Vern?"

"He doesn't own me. Even if he thinks so!" was her only comment, letting her body tense up against him. "I do what I want. When I want. How I want. With whom I like!"

He moved his hand up to her breasts. She squirmed convulsively, pushing up against his fingers. Then suddenly she forcefully pushed him away.

"Not *yet!*" she smiled, extending the rum bottle. "Not until we have a few drinks. Gotta have my rum—*first!* Rum before dum, dum?"

"Dum, dum?" he repeated, puzzled. She was truly amusing.

"The beat, beat, beat of the tom toms…you know like we're drums to beat out a jazzy rhythm and…I just love a hard throbbing…male animal!"

He chuckled and extended his glass.

"No, from the bottle," she told him. "Much

more…sexy that way. Don't you think? Not so formally…British!"

He gulped several swallows and then she followed his example, while he caressed her thigh.

"You're quite a joy," he told her in a husky low voice. "Coming at me like this!"

"I know! And it takes a real man to take me on!" was all she answered. Her words, strangely enough, sounded more like a daring challenge.

It was hard for him to believe she was here, offering herself so brazenly. In the last couple of weeks everybody had been just waiting out the voyage across the ocean, and then there were the plans to make and supplies to get. The loading of the yacht. Everything had been slow and easy because they knew they had a head start on the Henderson expedition.

And Ruby had played out her flirtatious games, which had seemed unlikely to end up like this. He was totally stunned, and delighted. In his English way and manner, Johnston was hardly a stuffy prude, in fact he was considered quite a rake back home.

"What are you thinking about?" she asked, nudging him with the bottle. "Have a swallow."

He swallowed and then reached for her. She resisted. "Not yet, my friend—we gotta finish the bottle! It's almost finished, anyway."

That was all right with him. He could wait after all this time. His eyes swept over her with hot desire. He was mentally caressing every inch of her body, wondering what she would look like, feel like, stark naked in his arms. And he was drunk enough not to care about anything else.

50

"If Vern saw you looking at me like that...oh, he'd beat the holy hell out of you," she laughed, delighted sounding. "You're making me feel naked all over! Love it!"

He felt an inner shudder run through him. He wouldn't want to tangle with the man. "Maybe we should be careful, then."

"Well, who's going to tell him? Not me!" She gulped on the bottle and then without warning gave it to him and in the same swift action unfastened her bra and pulled it over her head.

He sat there nearly paralyzed.

"Do I have to tell you what to do?" she cooed, leaning closer to him. Her lips parted and he watched as she moistened them with the delicate point of her tongue.

"Come on, love—show me what kind of an exciting real English brute beast you are!" she demanded, sliding her arms around his neck and moving her mouth down to his throat. "I love it wild, hard and demanding!"

He felt the sharp painful dig of her teeth as they clamped on his neck and then the moist nervousness of her tongue working between them. Suddenly she moved her mouth up to his.

A moment later they were locked violently together, her body grinding wildly against his, seeking tighter and harder contact. He felt her breasts under his fingers, moist with sweat.

"Take me..." she demanded starting to work with the front of his pants.

A moment later he had removed her shorts and they pressed closer together. "Now...now!" she moaned in his ear.

Just then there was a loud curse from the door-way.

"You dirty damn sons of bitches!" came Vern's voice.

Then Johnston felt Ruby yanked forcefully from him and a hard violent fist smash into his groin. The world spun into a horror of agonized pain that closed around his vision and flooded away all consciousness.

CHAPTER SIX

There wasn't much time for Dave Sheldon to think about making any friendly progress with Jean for the next couple of days. Everybody was busy with the last minute arrangements organizing their journey according to the Henderson's map. Then finally they started their way down the Amazon, and there wasn't much chance to pursue any possible relations with all the planning and the work that was taking place.

One afternoon, after they had been traveling the Amazon River for a little less than a week, he walked out on deck to see Jean stretched on a huge beach towel, barely covered by the smallest bikini he had ever seen a girl squeezed into.

Charlie was some twenty feet away, cleaning a rifle and staring lecherously at the full, curving lines of her figure. He nodded with a grin, and motioned Dave over.

"Have a swallow?" he asked, indicating the small pint of rum sitting next to him.

"None of that—right now." Dave commented in a low voice, glancing once more at the girl. "When did she come out?"

"Bout an hour ago, Davy-boy. I thought I'd lose my eyeballs."

"Henderson wants to see us—says something

came in on the radio a little while ago."

Charlie frowned and cocked his head to one side. "What the hell could be that important?"

"Don't know...but we better move."

The two of them walked past Jean. "Hi there, Jeannie-girl!" Charlie smiled.

She glared up at him, her face flushing under his lecherous gaze.

"Hello, Jean," Dave said softly, trying hard to keep from looking up and down her figure. He wanted to fairly devour her.

She squirmed, tensed under his swift examination.

"Hello!" she said in a slightly nervous tone of voice. Then she gave him a quick smile.

Some women would have simply shrugged it all off or flirted brazenly at that moment. Not Jean.

He followed Charlie down to the Captain's quarters.

"I don't see why he took her along on this dangerous trip!" grumbled Dave, stepping up to his friend.

"The Doc said she insisted—wanted to help him—she was too young for the first expedition...well you know how he is about her...doesn't want her left alone where men can have a chance to really make a woman out of her."

"A protective father, I suppose." Dave felt a stab of jealousy at Charlie's suggestion that any man should touch Jean. Any man, that is, except himself. Which was insane, considering she wasn't given him the time of day in that department. At least, not apparently so.

"Well, maybe she's not some virginal type! I

54

suspect she's just...a bit...snobbish! Any man would sure give a lot to get her. The moment I saw her, boy, did I wanted a piece of—"

"Drop it!" Dave snapped, annoyed far more than he wished to reveal.

Charlie glanced at him. "Okay. If you say so."

"I say so!"

Then the man chuckled. "I think you have a thing for her!"

"Fat chance," Dave admitted. "Anyway...there's a lot more to be concerned about...and a woman just complicates matters!"

There was a moment of silence, then Charlie laughed, shaking the rifle in his hand as they opened the Captain's door and walked in.

"Anyway," he said, "we're well equipped for anything that might come along. Plenty of this old fire power!"

"I see you finally made it." Henderson said in a tight sounding voice.

"You got only yourself to blame," Charlie told him.

The older man's eyebrows rose.

"Your daughter is a real stacked man-trap—especially in that bikini she's wearing," Charlie grinned.

Henderson's eyes narrowed and his jaw tightened. "I don't see what business that is of yours! Jean's here as a scientist and should be treated as one. She's not just another cheap woman that men can put their grimy hands on!" He paused for a moment, catching his breath and gaining some composure. "All I want understood...as far as Jean and you men are concerned—is that she's a scientist! Nothing else. So keep any other thoughts to yourself! Nothing more! Understand?"

Charlie just grumbled, shrugged as if he couldn't care less.

Dave held down his own anger. "Don't you think that's her business?"

"I think that you should keep your hands off her and your mouth shut!" There was an awkward silence and then Henderson finally relaxed. "That's not what I brought you here for. I have some news from Telbrook Island. Startling news!"

"What?" Dave darted out, knowing that it must have something to do with Ed Norton's death. Before they had left they'd been involved in a short investigation and then the police had given them the okay to leave. But Henderson had asked the island Commissioner to send them any information that might pertain to Norton or to themselves.

"It's better that I read it to you." Henderson arranged his glasses carefully and then looked down at the paper:

Dear Doctor,

I have distressing information for you. On the death of Ed Norton—those photos that were supposed to have been in his possession...they weren't found. Also, through our connections with most activities in the islands we discovered another interesting fact. The man you called Vern Yates has disappeared, along with his girl...a woman named Ruby—they left on a yacht owned by a

56

Mr. Johnston of England and captained by a Mr. Carver. We believe that they are headed for the same destination as you. Carver is known to be dangerous—though never caught directly in any crime. It is well known that he has been in on some messy deals in the past. Vern Yates as you know is deadly dangerous. He served ten years for a murder charge in France and was only let out because of a technicality....Be careful—whatever you do.

Your servant,

J. M. Brown,
Commissioner

"And so on." Henderson looked up at them, his face grim and set. "I don't like this. All we need is trouble. Maybe the Commissioner is wrong—but I don't think so. Vern Yates has a bad reputation as a treasure hunter who doesn't care about preserving things...just turning them into as much hard cash as possible and he's been after our information for a long time—as I told you before...that's the reason for all the double-foolery when Jean brought you two to me in the first place...but..."

"So—we got weapons!" Charlie Quinn announced, indicating the rifle he was now leaning on. "They're only human—and anyway, there should be enough loot for all of us...if it comes to that."

"Men like Yates won't share—they'll want it

all...and don't give a damn about the scientific issues. For me, this expedition is very much like the first one. For scientific purposes—for you two I realize that it's money. But remember; there is more than one way to make money from any discovery. We'll be doing it the careful and scientific way—it won't bring in as much, necessarily—but it will still be more than any one of us could ever spend in a lifetime. Yates is more likely to melt down the gold and take out the jewels and sell them at black market prices...and he doesn't know about the built-in booby traps—like the one that completely destroyed the other temple...whatever it was!"

"Where does this put us?" Dave demanded, feeling a sudden tight knot of fear run through him.

"In a race—I take it," Henderson commented dryly.

"Can't we get any more steam out of this crate?" Charlie asked, starting to work on the sights of his rifle.

"No—we just have to wait—and see what is open for us."

Dave worried about the pending trouble all the way up to the deck, but the moment he saw Jean stretched out on her beach towel, he forgot all about it.

Stepping over to her he sat down, silently staring at her.

She stirred slightly and then her eyes opened.

"What the...?" she gasped, jerking to an upright position. "How long have you been there?"

"Just a few minutes. I was admiring a beautiful woman."

A flush ran across her face and she turned away

58

slightly for a moment. Reaching for the pack of cigarettes on the towel next to her, she offered him one and then took one herself. He lighted them.

"I'm trying to stop," she said, nervously.

"What?"

"Smoking!" Then silence.

"What's keeping you from...stopping?"

She shrugged. "I do it when I'm nervous."

"I make you nervous?"

She shook her head, shrugged, glanced at him. Then looked away.

After a long, awkward silence she blew smoke out toward the nearer shore and then turned toward him.

She smiled briefly. "I've been giving you a hell of a time of it, haven't I?"

He nodded. "I understand...I guess. Just that you're...well, something nice!"

"Nice?" she smiled at the word, then at him. "Only nice?"

"Well...I don't think you'd like to know exactly what I'm thinking, now would you?"

"Maybe. Maybe not. Maybe I can guess," she offered, a little bit more in control. "I'm hardly...well...it is flattering."

She reached out an impulsive hand, touching his shoulder. "I really...well, just give me some time."

She paused and then looked down, took a puff of the cigarette in her hand and nervously turned back to him. "I...just don't know...this is serious business...this, I mean!"

She made a sweeping action of her arm to indicate the boat. "I guess I'm not much...good at social interaction. Not...never was the type to play around much. Pretty locked up in my studies and things like that. Dad's a hard act to follow."

"You need to do that? Follow him?"

"We're all we have. Really."

"You're a grown woman. Surely he realizes that you have a life of your own."

"He does. But we hold on to one another. When he was in Africa was I was pretty much involved in getting my degrees and all that…"

"Didn't date much?"

"Well, okay. I'm not a social butterfly but I'm not without…some experience. Just haven't had the time for fooling around."

"Who wants to fool around?" he countered, instinctively feeling that he sounded false.

The expression in her eyes as they met his at that moment, revealed her own take. "Don't all men want that kind of relationship with a lady?"

"I suppose…but not always."

"You make that…rather suggestive. Flattering. I suppose. But this isn't the time…or the place."

"This? Romantic tropical landscape? You gotta be kidding!" he quickly tossed off. Then shifting gears, not wanting to push her too far too fast, he added with a quick smile: "Forget it, for now. The main thing is that...well, we can be friends—at least!"

She laughed brightly and then looked out to sea. "I guess…why not—at least?"

There was a long silence after that, then she turned and looked at him. "You just don't understand what kind of life I've had…"

"Stop worrying," he told her. "It's not what happened in the past that counts—but rather what

60

you've become—today and tomorrow. Live in the present—not in the past. You're a grown woman. Don't be afraid to show your emotions and feelings. Express them..."

"Let's talk about something else."

"What?"

"The expedition?"

He thought that over. There were a few points he wanted to clear up in his mind about the whole thing, and there wasn't anybody better to talk to about it than Jean Henderson.

"A good idea," he told her, leaning back and trying to look casual. "Maybe you can tell me a few things that have been bothering me."

Her eyes narrowed, but she said: "Shoot."

"Well, from what I've learned so far...no! Let me put it this way." He paused, trying to collect and organize his thoughts. "Just exactly what is your father after? From what he's told me, he doesn't seem too interested in the money—and I can understand a little about the scientific end, but—well, what is it he's looking for? I get it is something totally different from mere scientific interest... What?"

"Atlantis."

"That has to be a lot of rot! Myths. Legends. Not hard reality."

Her face frowned, and her lips tightened. "Father doesn't fool with rot! He's a brilliant scientist—one of the top archaeologists in the world...he's always been interested in the lost continent idea. But his *scientific* knowledge would not allow him to really believe that there ever was any such place as Mu—a continent in the Pacific Ocean and Atlantis in the Atlantic. His endless search for lost cities led to that one he discovered in Africa with only the temple still standing. Yet, quite obviously, it was the remains of a once large outpost of prehistoric civilization. He now believes it to be, in many ways, more advanced than our own. That map he found—you haven't seen it, have you?"

Dave shook his head.

"Well, it's pretty primitive in the overall effect. But where cities are located, there is amazing detail—enough to make it possible for him to discover the general location of this one place we're going to."

"But how can he—? All that time...surely the world has changed and shifted

"Yes. The city in Africa and the one in South America have detailed markings. But even then it took time. The only way he could tell, for sure, was by a means of elimination. From what I understand about it there were only a few possible places it could have been, from the way the map is made. A valley completely surrounded by mountains which once had a river running through it along a narrow pass. Several things he had to have—like the valley had to be unknown—to civilization, that is. There just aren't too many places like it in South America. Not with all the conditions. I'm no dummy; but Dad's several leaps ahead of me! I don't know exactly how—but father has his own ways—scientific ways. And more than that...really. Some men instinctively know things; their minds can make fantastic leaps of logic and can travel down creative pathways the rest of us can't even imagine. Dad's like that!"

He considered everything she told him, then

said: "Yet from what you tell me—the map proves that there was this Atlantis and Mu—the two lost continents."

"No, not really," she admitted. "Well, not to anybody but Dad, who…like I said, sees things more vividly. And knows what he's talking about!"

"Then…what?" Dave exclaimed excitedly.

"Well, there's no record of any continents in the Pacific or Atlantic oceans at all on the map. But Dad claims it's the arrangement of everything…well, that's Dad!"

"Where does that leave us?"

"With a map that is unexplainable, that's all! Well, to us mortals, at least!" she stated matter-of-factly. "A map that couldn't possibly be made by a primitive society—unless they were great sailors and had explored the world."

"Is it possible to see this map?" Dave asked, wondering why he hadn't made any point to see it at the beginning. He'd just taken Henderson's word for everything. But then everything had happened so fast, and the fact that the older man was so well known throughout the world made it unnecessary to require proof of his word.

"I'm surprised you hadn't seen it before." She stood and indicated for him to follow her. "I'll take you down to the cabin and show you."

Lost City of the Damned, by Charles Nuetzel

CHAPTER SEVEN

Dave's heart started beating faster just at the thought of being alone in a cabin with Jean. All thoughts of the map were secondary as he watched the delightful sway of her hips as they swung with every step she took.

For some reason he had the idea that she was thinking thoughts very closely aligned with his. But *thinking* was one thing—and actually getting what he desired, quite another. At the same time he almost felt guilty entertaining such thoughts.

They moved into the passageway and then suddenly she turned into the Captain's quarters.

Much to his surprise there wasn't anybody else there. Deftly, she moved to the desk and opened the center drawer. Pulling out a large brown envelope she examined several photos and then took one out.

"Here—here it is," she said, looking up at him.

Their eyes met for a moment and he thought he saw a deep hidden desire flood past hers. Then it ebbed back to nothingness and they returned to their calm business expression. "Take a look if you want."

He moved over beside her and looked at the photo.

It was of a large wall with many designs around it. From what he could see, it didn't show anything.

"What the hell!" was his only shocked remark, "You're kidding?"

She smiled and then started outlining part of the pattern. And then he saw it slowly traced before his eyes the outlines of the western coast of Africa and then the East Coast of South America. It seemed incredible. Once one knew what to look for, the detail was amazing, especially considering that it may have been created several thousand years before Christ.

"What kind of race of people could have made—could have had all that knowledge?" he said breathlessly forgetting his physical hunger to make love to that beautifully sexual body standing so close to him.

"That's what father wants to find out That's why he's going there—why he always goes anyplace on the face of the world for the answer to where mankind came from –what our history is...and where civilization really started. Maybe he'll find the answer here."

"I still don't see how he could be sure where the damned city is!"

"Just have faith, my son!" Henderson's voice sounded from the doorway. "Just have faith in an old man's knowledge of a lifetime. I promise you all the fortune and riches you'll ever want."

For the first time since he had started on this expedition, Dave felt an inner shudder of apprehension. Regardless of all faith and trust, he was beginning to wonder what kind of deal he'd gotten himself into. Why was he so "lucky" to have been picked out of an unknown number of better-qualified people? Why was he a partner to this expedition into an unknown territory, to some ancient ruins that may or may not actually exist? Perhaps Henderson was quite mad. That made more sense than to believe his ancient Mu theories.

He looked down at the map once more. Now that Jean had pulled her finger away from the photo he found it next to impossible to retrace the outlines of the continents. Was it an old man's imagination? Had something happened to his mind because of the African trip? Maybe the temple and everything else was just the fantastic dream of a jungle-fevered brain.

Now, *that* made sense!

But what about the photos?

He pulled them out, one by one, from the envelope. As each in turn presented its image before his startled eyes he was forced to the conviction that these weren't fake. Yet could they really mean what he was being told they meant?

How could anybody really get a map out of that wall picture? An insane mind? A desperate imagination?

He shook his head in confusion, from side to side, not sure what to believe. Suddenly his world had been shattered violently.

A photo of a wall pattern that a scientist said was a picture of part of the world that led to a lost city that would have endless treasures.

He didn't know. Suddenly the whole thing seemed outlandishly fantastic. Dreamland invented in the perverse mind of an old man, half mad or...

Was it merely too fantastic to be anything but hard reality, the truth?

Slowly he put the pictures down and then, without a word, walked out of the cabin, outside.

Stunned, confused, not knowing what to believe any more, Dave just wanted to be alone to think it all out.

All he could do now was wait. It was too late to do anything but see the whole damn thing through.

One thing he did know: the other photos were authentic enough. Only the wall-map photo worried him. And that was the most important part of it all! But why fake it? Or, more to the point: how could Henderson fool himself to such a degree...?

He left that thought alone.

He couldn't help believing that they were on a wild goose chase, started by a scientist whose mind had cracked under the strain of too much work.

He'd have to talk to Charlie Quinn about it. He walked up on deck.

Gradually several things were beginning to bother him. And he had to work them out or discover the answers to them:

He spotted Charlie sitting in a chair working with his rifle.

Dave walked over and stopped in front of the other man. Now was as good a time as any...

* * * * * * *

The jungle was just damned hot, and Johnston hated every moment of it. There were heated tempers in their group and cross-currents of emotion were generating between everybody, threatening to explode in every direction at once. Ever since that day that Vern had caught him in the cabin bunk with Ruby, things had been getting heavier and thicker—

the only thing that held them together was the common goal: money! Each needed the other.

The only thing was that Vern Yates and Carver were beginning to work closely together, and that was the sign for Johnston to watch out for his life. The two men were at the head of the column, some distance away.

"What are you brooding about?" Ruby asked, stepping up beside him.

"Nothing," he grumbled, keeping his eyes fastened on the narrow newly cut trail before him.

They had been traveling in the jungle for more than a week. Sleeping out under the stars—and it was a lot of rot! He wasn't, by nature, an outdoorsman. Civilization was what rang his chimes. Good liquor, lovely, classy women and expensive eateries. And that good life cost plenty of money, which he didn't have in unlimited supply. He missed his house in England, his civilized comforts that he had been forced to give up for this wild chase into a tropical jungle. He'd invested a bundle.

"You're going to blow your lid if you don't let some steam out!" Ruby told him, her hip accidentally brushing his.

"Stop that!" he hissed in a low voice.

"I'm sorry—I didn't mean..." She mocked his whispering, winking seductively, obviously pleased with herself. "But I'm bored! Very bored..."

"You bitch—you meant it." He spoke softly so his voice didn't carry beyond the woman. "You'll get me killed yet."

"What's wrong—don't you know when a woman wants to be taken?" She whispered, voice softly with mocking. Then leaning even close, she whispered in his ear: "I wanna be with you, out here in the hot jungle...wouldn't you just *love* to finish what we started? I've thought of nothing else...oh, it would be—"

"Knock it off!" he retorted in a whisper. "I was drunk, then."

"Now you don't want me?" she giggled. "Bet you do."

"Please! Let's be smart!" he muttered, deciding not to deny his very intense interest in possessing this woman to the fullest. "So your hot! You know it. I know it. Everybody in the bloody world knows it!"

"Oh, how delicious! The whole bloody world knows about me! Do you think all those men want me as much as I want you?" she murmured softly, throatily, seductively, like a woman totally over-whelmed with desire. It was such a mockery of wanton desire that it would have been funny, under other circumstances. "I want you more now that we have tasted the hot fires...oh, now tell me...bet you want it, too."

"Shut up!" He glanced nervously at the front of the column where the other two whites were walking.

"Admit it." She brushed playfully against him, again. "I bet you're as hot...as I am!"

"Christ, Ruby!" he moaned, as her hand touched his shoulder, ran down his arm, caressingly. "What kind of game are you playing? You'll get both of us killed!"

"Hardly...hmmm...what a lovely word! Hardly...oh, so hardly! Love it!"

"Stop it, right now!" he ordered, finding it difficult to avoid shouting.

"Does it bother you?" she inquired. "My wanting you?"

"Hell, you don't *want* me. You just jump at any thing with pants on—and you know it!" he snapped, refusing to even look in her direction. "I've known plenty of…women in England…Europe…wherever—and I don't need danger city with you, love. I don't need a cheap whore!"

She laughed, quite obviously delighting in his description of her as a whore. "You don't pull punches, now do you?"

"I don't think I need to. Not with you!" He was feeling just a little less annoyed.

"Me neither!" she slipped close, her hand reaching down to his inner thigh, brushing along it in a very brazenly intimate way. "Me neither, big boy!"

"Damn it. You bloody slut!" he cursed, hitting her hand away from him. "You could drive a man to rape! Bloody damned whore!"

"Vern would make you sorry you said that—if he learned about it," she snapped back, almost viciously.

He stopped suddenly, a sickness icing its way through his whole nervous system. "You wouldn't tell him!"

She laughed tauntingly. "Oh, wouldn't I?"

Her eyebrows arched and she smiled seductively at him. "You never can tell what I might do. After all…I'm just a cheap, sluttish whore in heat! You can't trust me to play by any fine British Lady's rules! Now, can you?"

Cursing, he moved away, quickly stepping up to the head of the single column of native barriers where Vern Yates and Carver were conversing.

"How much further to this damned city?" he demanded, still hearing Ruby's taunting laugh in the background over the chanting and singing of the hundreds of birds and insects which moved all around them in the jungle.

"Damned, if I know. This blasted map doesn't say much. All I understand is that we gotta follow this dead riverbed to its end. Maybe those mountains we saw yesterday in the distance."

"Well, damn it all! Keep Ruby off my back!"

Vern gave him a strange angry look but said nothing. But that one glance held the threat of murder.

They were a nice bunch of slobs out looking for a lost city that might not even exist, for all Johnston knew. The quicker everything was finished, the better.

Chapter Eight

The Henderson expedition had entered the jungle at the mouth of a narrow river, leaving the yacht where it could be docked, with a small crew of men. On the surface, it seemed that everything was running smoothly; and for the most part it was. Only, in Dave Sheldon's mind things were in a twisted distortion. The heat, the timid front that Jean Henderson presented to him—coupled with his own doubts about the destination's reality—all tended to create an uncertain cloud over every day, deepening as the days continued.

It was night now, and as he lay back on his sleeping bag looking up through the trees at the night sky, Dave felt a keen edge of nervous excitement rush through him. He didn't quite know why, at first.

Then he recognized the scent. The light perfumed fragrance of Jean Henderson.

Quickly he turned and looked behind him. She was standing there in the darkness, looking at him in a strange way. When she saw that he noticed her, she started, stiffening.

"What are you doing there?" he asked in a surprised voice.

"It's a free world!" she snapped, hurt sounding, then turned and started to move away.

He stood and after strapping on his holstered army .45, he moved to her. "Wait a moment—"

She paused but didn't turn.

Moving up to her, he reached out and turned her around. Her whole body was rigid and stiff.

He relaxed and his arms fell to his sides. For a moment they stood there, looking at each other. With every second the hungry desire worked tighter and tighter inside Dave until he almost found it impossible from reaching out for her.

She was wearing a loose-fitting shirt, partly open in front, tucked in tight around her waist. The jeans were skin-fitting, accenting the, full curve of her legs and thighs.

Her lips were half-parted as if she were in some kind of spell.

Nervously he reached for a pack of cigarettes and then lighted one. He extended the pack to Jean, but she just shook her head slowly from side to side.

For some reason there didn't seem to be anything to say. Each just silently seemed to be taking in the other. It was one of those moments when people don't really have any need for words. The night and the surroundings were enough communication for them both. Yet the quiet meaning was allusive.

He puffed lightly on his cigarette and then silently motioned her to follow him as he started off into the surrounding jungle.

"Don't go too far in," she murmured, "it can be dangerous."

He just shook his head. He only wanted to get away from the others, even though they were asleep. Alone with Jean Henderson for a few moments, to

74

take advantage of the mood which held her captive and more easily bending to a friendly attitude. For a while, at least, the fear had left her eyes and only a half-dreamy expression veiled her thoughts.

After a few seconds, when they were some 50 feet away from the campsite, he turned and moved closer to her. For an instant he almost drew her into his arms, but something held him back. Not her expression or anything like that—rather something within him that wanted to be sure about her desires. Being too forward could be counter-productive.

With any other woman the next move would have been obvious. But with Jean he simply didn't know.

All at once he felt like a small school kid, standing in front of a young girl for whom he had an overwhelming crush.

"So much is happening," he said lamely, taking another deep drag from his cigarette. "I mean...well..."

"Yes...things are happening, I suppose." She half smiled, the corners of her lips dimpling. "A puzzle, that. Things happening."

"You're mocking me," he accused.

"No. Really. Not!" Her voice, though, was thick with amusement. She enjoyed having the upper hand. His discomfort must have been nakedly obvious.

"Yes, you are," he countered, a bit annoyed, and at the same time charmed by the glint of amusement in her eyes.

"Well, as you were saying ... now, what was it you were saying?"

He stared at her for some moments, fighting the

desire to just yank her into his arms and smother those soft lips with passionate kisses.

She remained silent, just staring evenly back at him, waiting. It was totally unnerving.

"What I'm trying to say is…" He stumbled over the words, not even sure what he wanted to say. He could hardly express his real feelings, his desire for her, his ever-growing mad hunger for this woman who was so distant and cool to any advances. "Darn, Jean. I can't think straight!"

"I guess not, apparently. Just a little boy lost for words!" she softly laughed. "Rather…appealing in its way."

"Damn!"

"And swearing, too. My, my. Naughty boy!" She openly laughed. "I'm sorry."

"For what?"

"Laughing."

"Well…I guess that's better then crying!"

"I suppose so," was her only comment.

"What, the hell, are we talking about?" he exploded.

"You got me, Dave." There was softness in the way she said his name that almost lingered over it, caressingly. It was almost intimate.

He started to lean towards her, then just a flickering of her eye-lids warned him. He backed off, and she relaxed.

"I'm only human," he managed.

"Okay," was all she said to that.

"Do you mind?"

"What?"

"Well, you know…never mind. Oh, hell!" The words sounded lame, even to him. "You have me tongue-tied. Like a silly little boy."

"No way! Speak up, and say anything you like."

For a moment he was tempted. "I wouldn't dare!"

"Why not?" she murmured, glancing away, looking out across the night sky. "Are you afraid?"

"I think I am," was all he could say for a moment, then added, "do you mind?"

She just shook her head slowly from side to side.

They were silent for a very long time, each caught in their own thoughts. He tried, several times, to open the conversation, but choked down the words before they could be formed.

Finally he decided on a safe subject.

"You know how far inland we have to go?" He knew the answer, but was desperately seeking something to talk about.

"No—nobody knows for sure. Just follow this river bed—until we reach the valley with a white-capped mountain."

She was looking off into the jungle blackness, as if she were afraid to let her eyes meet his. "It seems incredible that we are really here..."

"Yes." He was thinking more about the fact that they were finally alone together—that seemed incredible too.

She was very near, near enough to reach out and pull close to him. The creamy whiteness of her beautiful throat was throbbing with life and passion. Her chest was rising and falling heavily. The moment was right, yet for some reason he found it impossible to reach for her. That slap she had given him the evening he'd tried to kiss her was still too vivid in his memory.

In the jungle there were the sounds of night, the growl of savage animals—the distant moan of a cougar. Then suddenly without warning the snarl of one of the South American jungle cats sounded above them in the tree.

Jean screamed and leaped closer to him. In that frantic moment he was torn between running, taking her in his arms, and ravishing her, and pulling the Army .45 out of the holster at his side. Logic and sanity dictated what he must do.

Then both of them were tumbling backwards to the ground. The weight of Jean's struggles had thrown them off balance.

He saw out of the corner of his eye the flashing black leap of the cougar as it flew through the air over their heads and landed on the ground.

Desperately he reached for his gun. As the cat turned toward them, ready for a second leaping attack, he aimed and fired.

Dave was aware of three things at once: The pressure of Jean's body next to him heating the already deep need for her; the snarling fury of the cougar; and his careful cool-headed aim and then squeezing the trigger.

It seemed as if time stood still for a moment. The cat stood there poised for the leap, frozen in space and time. And then the exploding sound of the gun and the cat gave a startled jerk, a quick turn and then the animal disappeared into the jungle night, leaving them alone.

He had no way of knowing if it had been wounded or just scared off—but one thing he could be thankful about; it had caused Jean Henderson to come into his arms even if it was a frantic move for her own survival.

Now he turned his attention to her. She was leaning against him, lying half across him. He had one arm around her shoulder. Everything was just right for one explosive kiss. They were alone, lying in each other's arms, each breathing heavily, each aware of the nearness of the other.

He pulled her closer and she didn't resist, but instead surged tighter against him. A sigh uttered past her teeth as their lips met. He felt the heavy beating of her heart.

Just then the sound of Doctor Henderson's voice interrupted them.

"Jean—Sheldon! Where are you? Where are you?"

It sounded frightened and concerned.

She smiled helplessly at Dave, and for a moment it seemed as if she wasn't willing to let her father know where they were; then she slowly moved away from him.

"Over here, Dad," she called.

"Are you safe?"

"Yes," Dave told the scientist, standing, and then helping Jean to her feet. He felt angry with Henderson, even though he realized that there wasn't any reason to take it out on the man. Yet his jaw tightened as he saw the deadly cold expression on her father's face.

"What happened?" Henderson demanded, glancing over at Dave, his jaw set in hateful violence. He seemed to know what had happened. He could forgive Jean, but not Dave, and he showed that in the icy look of anger he shot once more at Sheldon.

Then Jean started explaining about the cougar.

Dave turned and walked off. The voices faded out as he entered the camp.

CHAPTER NINE

During the day it rained at least once—at night it was chilly. That was the Amazon jungle. And it was the world in which the two parties moved, cutting their way across a virgin, almost untouched land where only the feet of head-hunters had ever passed. Two white groups, treading through unexplored wilderness—one of the few places in the world which was still virtually unexplored.

But they moved and progressed and cut their way through the underbrush not unseen. Eyes watched and waited. They looked and wondered and stared, savagely and murderously—waiting for the right moment to strike.

* * * * * * *

Henderson and Sheldon were talking quietly under the shade of a tree near the bank of the small stream that they had been following for several days.

Jean watched them from the place she was bathing. She was far enough away to be safe from searching and eager male eyes, but close enough so that she could see them anxiously arguing over some point or other. It seemed as if they had been on each other's backs for several days now. Ever since that evening when she had fallen into Dave's arms and the cougar had leaped at them.

This was the first time she'd had to take a real bath for at least three days and it felt so good to feel clean for a moment, at least. To soap off all the dirt and sweat. Every muscle in her ached, both from the exercise of daily walking through the jungle and from something else that she didn't like to admit even to herself.

An inner thrill rushed through her as she remembered the delight of that kiss. How she had wanted it, ever since she had first met Dave Sheldon at gunpoint. In a way, thinking back to that day, it was rather silly of her to have brought them to her father that way, yet they hadn't really known what type of men Dave and Charlie were. Only had Norton's word for it, and he was dead. Plus she'd never liked that man very much. So it took her a while to trust his two friends. She still wasn't completely certain about either of them. Sure, Dave was a wild card—and a bit frightening. Desire was one thing, but she didn't trust men. Experience had taught her to be careful. A nasty love affair had made her bitter and very frightened of getting involved with a man again. But all that had happened a couple of years ago. She didn't want to think of Allen. That man had soured her, but good.

Jean turned her mind away to other thoughts and tried to center on the feel of the water surging around her naked skin; it was cooling in the hot, humid jungle.

Suddenly she heard a rustling in the bushes. Startled, she looked up, and her eyes came level with Charlie Quinn's who was standing on the shore staring at her.

He laughed. Winked. Grinned lustfully.

"What're you doin', baby?" he asked as she quickly dipped downward into the water to hide her nudity.

"What are *you* doing?" she demanded in an angry voice. "Get out of here!"

"Oh, come on." He sounded playful, jokingly putting her on. "Don't tell me that you ain't been in the raw in front of a man before."

"That's none of your damn business!" she cried. "Get out of here! And now!"

"Can't a man enjoy a little fun?" He laughed in open delight. "What's the harm?"

"You've been drinking!" As usual.

"Just a mite!" Charlie Quinn admitted, winking. "But not enough not to enjoy the beauty of a naked woman! Especially you. What a sight. What a joy! You'd make any man."

"Oh, stop. Right now!"

"Don't ya like a little kiddin'?"

"That's not kidding. It's insulting! Coming from you … like that!"

"What's wrong with me, baby?"

"You're drunk. And hardly a gentleman!"

"I'm drunk and hardly a gentleman. You're right!" His eyes fairly devoured her.

"Oh go away!" she exploded, turning from him.

There was a moment of silent, followed by a sudden intake of breath from the man.

"God, lady. You're somethin' else!"

"Go away!" she told him, without looking in his direction. "Leave me alone!"

"The hell, I will!" he chuckled. Then she heard

the noise of clothing being taken off and turned to look over her shoulder.

"You aren't bathing here!" Totally alarmed she told him.

His shirt was off and he was beginning to work with the buckle of his pants. "What do you think? The river ain't owned just by you, now."

"Go some other place!"

"Why?"

"Damn it all!" she cursed, starting to swim downstream away from him and toward her father and Sheldon.

Charlie Quinn laughed, diving in after her.

"You can't get away from me," he laughed.

Frightened, she swam faster, attempting to out-distance him. She couldn't stand the idea of his creepy hands even touching her.

For weeks, now, he had been giving her glances that were brimming over with animal lust. She knew his type, and under normal circumstances would have not been too much concerned. But this wasn't a civilized world. And the man was probably half-drunk. And she was the only woman around!

Suddenly she felt fingers clamping around her ankle and pulling her backwards. She tried to scream, but her head dipped under water before any sound could be made.

Desperately she fought to be free, kicking out at Charlie, frantically trying to hit him with her fists, while at the same time struggling to surface and scream for help.

Thrashing and kicking, she attempted to raise her head above water. Her lungs were bursting in pain and agony. She didn't know if she was more terrified of drowning or Charlie.

Desperately she kicked out at him; attempting to reach the surface of the water

Then suddenly, as she twisted violently away, and at the same time pushed her foot into his face, she felt air suck into her lungs.

A scream of terror broke past her lips.

She heard an answering yell from the shore and then she felt Charlie's hands releasing her and she was suddenly alone.

Under the water she saw the shadowy form of Quinn swimming away. On the shore Dave Sheldon and her father were frantically looking in her direction.

"What's wrong?"

She thought for a moment and then shook her head. It was best to keep things quiet concerning Charlie—as long as she could keep him under control. Chances were he'd learned his lesson, she decided.

"I was just startled by a fish," she lied, realizing that it wouldn't do the temper of the group any good if her father and Dave knew about her ordeal with Charlie.

Things were difficult enough.

Slowly, she started swimming back to where she had been bathing. She took her time, waiting to see Quinn step out of the stream and then quickly get dressed and disappear into the surrounding forest.

Maybe nothing else would happen. Maybe Quinn would take this as a warning—she hoped so. She didn't want any trouble. Least of all from a man like him.

Finally she reached the shore where her clothing

was. She walked out of the water and started dressing.

For some reason she had the sickening feeling that Charlie Quinn wasn't the type of person to just try once and then quit. She felt there would be other times—more heated and more forceful—and more dangerous. Maybe she should make sure she was armed.

Pulling her bra around her breasts she sighed, tired. Then her panties slipped on and after a moment a skirt and blouse followed. She started off, back toward the campsite.

She hadn't gone twenty feet into the jungle before she came face to face with Charlie Quinn!

* * * * * * *

Dave Sheldon returned with Henderson to the shade of the tree and took up the photo map, pointing to where both of them believed they were presently located. "Then this means just about three or four more days—" Dave said.

Henderson nodded.

"Where, the hell, are the mountains the valley indicated on this map?" Dave demanded, still finding it hard to actually see the outlines of any map in the jumble of lines and criss-crosses which made up the endless pattern in the photo."

"They'll be there, believe me."

"How can you be sure?"

"For one thing, the temple wall was in color and that told me exactly what to look for—the photo that Norton had...that I assume the Yates party now has in its possession...was marked up like this." Hender-

86

son took out a pencil and started making lines and shadings on the photo that had been printed on dull paper. After a moment Dave was shocked to see sketched out before him in striking detail the coastlines of both Africa and South America.

"Millions of years ago, the world was a different place. The continental drift theory is now accepted as hard fact. That, of course, has little to do with our human history …but, well, you have to understand that at one time, Africa and South America were one solid land mass, either connected tightly—or as I sometimes have the feeling—loosely, broken by rivers and lakes and seas. That's the reason I've started on this whole thing in the first place. Believe me, there has been more time and effort put into researching these issues than you could imagine before I contacted Norton. Months of details, night and day…years, actually."

This was the first time that Dave and Henderson had really gotten around to talking seriously about where they were going.

"This thing I'd like to know—even if it is slightly belated—just how were you able to know—or rather, feel, so sure that there is anything left of the city?"

Henderson shook his head from side to side. "I'm not going out as blindly as you—"

"No—no, that's not it, Doctor. I went blindly into this whole deal because of your reputation—and I'll admit that I've been having doubts now and then—but—well go on, please."

"The way it's handled is to search out legends and superstitions. Myths, if you will. Anything that can be considered sound, reasonable, factual. Well, okay, factual might be a bit strong, say supported by enough hard evidence to be suggestive…legends and mythology come out of distant, vaguely remember historical events, lost in time. Well, anyway, you have to start somewhere. If you can't believe in the evidence, then you find evidence you can believe in. Then you compare locations and geological history in the surrounding territory. In this case it was a fairly simple matter. Only a couple of indicated cities. All the others were either destroyed by civilization's march or by geological disruptions in the past. I believe that this one may still exist.

"The territory we're entering tomorrow has hardly been touched by civilized man. It is one of the few places in South America which is still virtually unknown."

"Then how do you know about—"

"Geologic shiftings?"

Dave nodded. But that was more bluff than anything else; since the other man's words were still rather baffling.

"By the surrounding territory which *is* known. Believe me, the less you worry about—"

At that point there was a scream, interrupting their conversation.

Jean Henderson's voice cried out again in terror.

Both the Doctor and Dave stood, startled. Then they started rushing toward the sound of the voice. Dave drew his .45 from the holster at his side as he pushed through the jungle.

* * * * * * *

The moment Jean Henderson saw Quinn a startled but muffled scream sounded from her throat. She was surprised and slightly terrified. He had been waiting for her, standing there, just waiting.

"What, the hell?" Charlie cursed, bitterly, stepping closer and trying to calm her down.

"Don't touch me!" she choked, moving back. But he continued to follow her.

"Please—leave me alone!" she pleaded, raising her arms out in front of her. "Please!"

Charlie had paused, a shocked expression on his face. He was looking past her, over her shoulder.

She turned...and screamed.

Standing there, watching them, were half a dozen Indians. The leader had a thin bone stabbing through his nose—all of them were naked except for loin cloths and knives and spears. They were looking eagerly at her body, their eyes fascinated by her white skin.

One of them said something to the other in a mumbled unintelligible tongue. The other nodded and *laughed,* pointing his spear in her direction.

She screamed again, rushing toward Quinn. It was the lesser of two dangers. Charlie was basically a friend—natives were more enemy and deadly than Quinn's normal male sexual hunger.

Just then Henderson and Dave Sheldon pushed through the underbrush, each holding a gun in his hand.

Her father came to an abrupt stop at her side, raising his hand to bring Sheldon to a halt.

"Let me handle this," he told the others, stepping carefully forward.

Lost City of the Damned, by Charles Nuetzel

CHAPTER TEN

Ruby had been feeling a burning ache for a man ever since they had hit the jungle; yet Vern hadn't once made any attempt to make love to her. The longing for a man was grating her nerves raw to the point where she didn't give a damn, anymore.

She had always needed a healthy serving of sex, even as a teenager. As a fully matured, experienced woman, it was impossible to control her unrelenting hungers—unlike most women, she craved sex like men did. Maybe more so.

Why Vern hadn't touched her was impossible to tell. And she didn't care why—she just wanted it.

It must be the jungle heat—or something, she thought, nervously stepping up to the fire where Vern was sitting warming himself.

It was early evening and both Carver and Johnston were out of the camp, hunting. She and Vern were alone because the Indian bearers had gone with the other two. She hoped that they would catch something—but that they would also take a long time doing it.

Moving close to Vern, she slipped her arms around his neck from behind and then covered his eyes with her hands.

"Guess *who?*" she asked.

"Damn it all, Ruby—cut that out!"

"What's wrong?" she demanded, stepping around to the front of him on the other side of the small fire. "You haven't so much as touched me."

He gave her a nasty grin. "Why? Why should I—you're just a hot little tramp…who doesn't care where she gets it—"

She held down the biting anger in her chest. It was painfully true. Right then, she didn't care how or who she got it from—she needed someone.

"You better take me while you still can!" she warned him.

"I'll take you when I get good and ready. And not before!

"I need it!" she stated almost matter-of-factly.

"I know that," he laughed, nastily, letting his eyes sweep along her body, pausing where the blouse was unbuttoned at the top to give a generous view of her fleshy breasts. "That's what you get screwing around with that Johnston guy."

His eyes lingered at the dip at her neckline and she leaned forward, slightly, in order to give him an even better view. For a moment she saw desire spark in his face. "But there are other—more important things to think about!"

She raised her fingers to the top of the blouse and yanked it open.

"Come on, Vern!" she almost snarled, wanting to claw her way into his arms. "Stop the crap!"

"Cut it out, baby—not today!"

Furiously, she threw herself at him, flinging her arms around his head and pressing herself tight against him. He could hardly deny her lush body; the greedy need welling up inside her.

"Please," she moaned in his ear.

92

Abruptly he yanked her closer and with one savage pull ripped her bra off and brutally clawed at her breasts as his lips savagely covered hers. It was a demanding, bestial assault, just as she loved it.

A convulsive shudder flooded across Ruby as he forced her back on the ground.

She was trembling uncontrollably by now.

She couldn't even speak, was only able to make murmuring sounds that begged for him to ravish her.

But the man suddenly pulled away and got up. A cruel laugh broke from his throat, as he looked down at her, with both hands on his hips.

"Now you know how it is to be tormented!" He turned from her and started moving away.

A cry of insane frustration exploded from her lips as she gathered herself up and sprang toward the man. Leaping on his back, she clawed, bit and kicked at him, and would have driven a knife up and down his spine if she'd had one in her hand at that moment.

"You no good...bitch!" he cursed, twisting, around and throwing her off him. Then his fist doubled and he swung. Just as suddenly his arm came to a stop—freezing in mid-air. His eyes fastened on something behind her.

"Okay, Mister Yates," Johnston's voice sounded. "You can stop right where you are."

* * * * * * *

The leader looked at Henderson and then at Quinn. His savagely cruel face was deadly serious and his mouth tightly drooping. He grumbled something to the other natives with him.

Henderson started making motions and actions with his hands and face.

The savage looked at him for a long time, then he started waving his arms, and speaking rapidly.

There was a mumbling among all of the head-hunters and after a moment, once Henderson waved them to follow him, they stepped in behind the white-haired scientist.

All this time Jean leaned against Dave, and he couldn't help noticing the way she trembled slightly as the savages stepped by her.

"Take it easy, kid," he told her, smiling and placing an arm impulsively around her shoulder.

She looked up at him and a thin smile worked the corners of her lips and her eyes seemed to express their thanks for the comfort.

After a moment Quinn followed after the head-hunters. The look he gave Jean and then Dave made the latter wonder just what had been going on before the savages had come on the scene. Quinn could be a brute with women; but basically harmless if handled right.

He looked at Jean, but she said nothing; instead, stepped away from him and started following the others.

In a few moments they were in the camp, and Henderson was talking to the leader through one of the Indian bearers who knew the head-hunters' language.

After a few moments of conversation, Henderson pulled out several necklaces of bright beads from his package, which he had brought on the trip for just this sort of a purpose.

The savage eyes of the Indian head-hunters brightened wildly. Their hands reached for the trinkets, eagerly taking them like starved children grabbing for candy.

After a moment of excited gibbering they filed out of the clearing, disappearing into the surrounding foliage.

The Doctor sighed a breath of relief and turned toward Dave and Jean.

"Head-hunters," was his only word.

"You're kidding," Dave exploded. He'd guessed the obvious, but when the other man said those words out loud it had startled him. A light shudder of revulsion moved across his spine.

"The Amazon used to be full of them—most of them are civilized nowadays, more or less—but in this territory, I don't know. They were friendly enough, though, as long as you know how to treat them."

"Now what?" Dave wanted to know, looking around at the jungle.

"Watch and wait and pray a little, I guess. If they aren't still practicing their 'art' there's a chance we won't be bothered by them again, unless we get in their way."

"Wouldn't it be safer to turn back?" Charlie grumbled. "I'm attached to my head!"

"No!" Jean cried. "You lost your head, already!"

The man's eyes snapped towards her, alarmed. Then as their gaze met, he understood the silent warning and merely nodded.

Henderson shook his head from side to side, as he was saying: "We must have been in their country for a couple of days now—otherwise they wouldn't have shown themselves. Turning back wouldn't help us if they're interested in collecting our heads—so we might as well push on. After all we didn't expect to have a free ride all the way."

"And we came fully supplied for any kind of trouble," Dave pointed out. "I assume! That is."

"We better pull camp—it's about time that we started out...anyway," Henderson told them. "Just a couple more days and we'll know what we came all this way to find."

"Just a couple more days," Dave thought, and he'd know either how rich he was—or if Henderson was mad.

He couldn't help wondering about the other group of whites who were headed for the same destination. What kinds of people—and what kind of clash would the groups have? Therein lay serious danger.

It could be deadly—that much he knew...

Unless the Yates group got lost in the jungle—which was fairly likely, considering that the only thing that was keeping this group from getting completely lost was Doctor Henderson.

He shook himself, trying to push the thoughts out of his mind.

Instead, think of Jean, he told himself.

Beautiful Jean and that one kiss and embrace the other evening in the jungle. The warm and electric feel of her. The full supple eager body had stretched against his, hungry and passionate and anxious.

He looked across the clearing to where she was starting to help break camp.

He wondered when they would be alone again, when they would have a second chance to go into each other's arms...

He hoped it would be soon. It had to be soon. Or it might never happen.

LOST CITY OF THE DAMNED, BY CHARLES NUETZEL

CHAPTER ELEVEN

The valley waited, like it had been waiting for thousands of years—in silence and mystery— awaiting the touch of modern man.

It was a small valley, aged and savage, rugged and virgin except for the crumbled ruins at its further end, under the lonely high snow-capped mountain. One large peaked building was surrounded at every turn with rubble that may have once been a great city. But there was no obvious hint about what it may have looked like; nor that it had even existed. Time had wiped the evidence level of any details. Only the mysterious temple now stood, waiting for the intruders. How it has survived was a secret yet to be discovered—and maybe never to be revealed. Now it was waiting like a magnificent monument of a dead age; of a vanished civilization that once had been powerful and advanced beyond the world which had slowly surrounded it and finally, over the years watched it die and all but fade into crumbling dust.

Natives had, for centuries, wondered and puzzled over this place—and remained safely distant, not daring to approach.

Nobody knew its origins; only legend and myths hung around it like some invisible mist clouding the long lost details of its wonder and glory.

The head-hunters had developed wild stories around this strange valley. They believe their genesis was hidden in the rubble of the once proud civilization that must have existed here. But all this had been there long before their arrival. Still, they blindly believe in the ancient warning that stopped them from approaching it under any circumstances.

The legend claimed that anyone who entered might die—anyone who went into the sacred temple would *die a horrible death.*

But what did primitive natives know? What could they possibly know about such ancient truths that may have been swallowed up in, perhaps, thousands of years before their earliest ancestors had come to these jungle lands of modern South America?

CHAPTER TWELVE

An undercurrent of excitement overshadowed the murderous hate developing in the Yates' expedition. Greed for money was stronger than the jealous pressure of passion and lust. Even Ruby apparently had lost her driving need for a man once they entered the valley.

Johnston had been moody ever since they had started out on the jungle trip. The continued flirting which Ruby had flashed his way had caused deep repercussions to move through him, which he wasn't quite able to handle. That afternoon, when he'd returned to camp early from hunting he had found Vern and Ruby fighting. He didn't care what it was about, or who had caused it. The only thing that had mattered was that Vern was about to hit a woman, and that was one thing he couldn't put up with.

He'd just automatically pointed his gun.

But the murder in Vern's eyes had only brought to the surface the basic fact that the only thing, which held the group together, was the common need of each for the other to satisfy their personal greed.

Now that they were finally within a few hours of their destination, even that moody feeling grew shallow compared to their mounting passionate excitement to get what they had come for and to see this legendary marvel.

A lost city.

Johnston was walking next to Ruby. They didn't touch each other, even though she was staying fairly close to him. Ever since her blow-up with Vern, Yates made it a point to keep his distance. But now all four of them were walking fairly close together. They were following a narrow overgrown game trail, their Indian bearers moving in a long line behind them, while several choppers cutting the trail ahead free of loose vines.

All of a sudden there was a shout from ahead; then one of the men came running up, his eyes wide with terror. He was shouting a lot of double talk that Johnston couldn't understand. Before he could try to explain, he fell forward, a small shiny golden dart imbedded in his back.

There was a scream of horror from the men behind them and both Carver and Yates dove forward on their stomachs.

Johnston instantly pulled his rifle from his shoulder and started to move forward.

"What the hell happened?" he asked the second bearer who had been chopping the trail ahead of them. The man was standing stiffly, looking wide-eyed at him, his mouth hanging open, his face distorted in pain. He didn't say anything.

That's when Johnston noticed the large, ugly hole in the other's chest, blood-covered and gaping.

Touching the man with his gun, he watched grimly as the body dropped downwards to the ground.

"What is it?" Carver demanded behind him,

102

from the ground.

He turned. "I think some..." His voice trailed off. His brain suddenly registered something that it had missed because of the native's body.

He turned and looked ahead at the trail that had abruptly come to an end. Blinking, he tried to focus his eyes. They weren't fooling him.

Standing before him was a massive door, made of some hard, weathered metal. It was carved and etched with flowing designs and strange pictures.

He just stood there, stunned, unable to believe his eyes.

They had finally reached their destination!

But, he realized that *it was a booby-trapped destination.*

He stepped forward carefully, not touching anything, just seeking a closer look. But accidentally his rifle scraped the wall, hitting a projecting carving which instantly gave under the pressure.

Without warning, the world opened underneath him and he was spinning downwards, and then blackness folded around him as his feet came to an abrupt stop, his body caving in on his legs.

* * * * * * *

The pressure of keeping their eyes open for any signs of more head-hunters kept Dave from having time for more than mere conversation with Jean or Charlie. Still, Jean kept as near to him and as far from Quinn as she possibly could. Because of that, Dave couldn't help feeling that something had happened between them which made her a little afraid of the other man.

A couple of times they saw the head-hunters, but never any sign of the other group which was reportedly headed for the lost city, too.

"The jungle's big," Henderson had told him once when he had commented on the subject. "Also, the river. No doubt, they had a smaller boat and were probably able to go down the narrower river where we left our yacht." He had gone on to explain the complete lack of evidence of any more whites within a hundred miles of them.

The pressure and tension were building and also the excitement. The idea of finding the remains of an ancient civilization which had existed long before his own—then vanished—left him with so many mixed emotions that it was hard to keep his mind focused on the personal fortune that he was seeking.

"What, exactly, do you—I mean what kind of civilization do you think built the temple in Africa? And this one? Do you think the same peoples built both of them?" he asked Henderson one afternoon as they were starting up the low range of mountains which both felt must be the ones that would lead to the valley where the lost city was located.

"That, I will only be able to speculate on," the Doctor told him. "It could be remains of some Atlantian culture—or some highly civilized seafaring culture which had spanned the distance between Africa and South America. If—as might be possible—the two continents were at one time joined—or much closer than they are today—it wouldn't really be so incredible. I suppose. Though somewhat doubtful, of course."

"In just a few thousand years how could the

continents drift so far—?"

"Who knows? I doubt it, but..." The man shrugged, vaguely. "And who knows for sure, if it *was* only a few thousand years before—or, for that matter, that a human intelligence built it?"

"You're kidding!" Dave exclaimed in a shocked voice. "Aliens from outer space, I guess you'll be suggesting?"

"Not really. Only pointing out that there is no proof of anything much connected to these ideas of mine. The past is a tangled mystery, and things may have existed far beyond our ability to imagine. I don't even like to build theories on...speculation. But...I positively know that we'll find something well worth the effort it takes. Think. A lost city with metal doorways—"

"You never mentioned that before!" Dave said excitedly.

"I didn't? Sorry." The older man smiled gently. "So many things on my mind the last few years...I don't know—maybe it's not really so amazing really—considering that they had gold and made beautiful statues like the one you saw in the photos. They weren't carved—*they were made in molds.*"

Just then Jean stepped up and took hold of Dave's arm. "What are you two men talking about—can't you give a girl a little time?"

That broke up the conversation and it now drifted in other directions which had little to do with lost civilizations or money or even romance. But he kept turning this information over in his mind. His head was spinning, unable to absorb the implications. As a child, he'd read things by Shaver and by Hubbard and many other science fiction writers who suggested all types of wild histories under other worldly connections in the past and into the future. They were all fused together by creative writers' minds inventing half-realities out of half-baked theories and suppositions. Where make-believe broke off from real fact was sometimes difficult to define. Churchward's book on Mu, written in the 1800s, gathered together endless bits of undefined evidence of strange ancient cultures and blended them into a theory of a sunken continent that mysteriously disappeared under the Pacific Ocean. Some people faithfully believed the "evidence" in his books. Others mocked writings such as these as con-jobs fostered onto the gullible public. Even religious movements had come out of unknown secret tablets and golden documents that somehow had vanished. Where did truth and fact end and where did it turn into wild science fiction fantasy?

And their trip into the jungles of South America in search of a lost city would, perhaps, blur the lines between reality and make-believe even further. If they found some ruin to support the doctor's theories, what could anyone believe, then, about our known human history?

Now they were approaching the valley, and the suspense that had been building up all these weeks was finally flooding over to a tension that draped over all of them. The waiting for the head-hunters, the possible signs of the other group.

It was at the base of the valley floor that they found their first clues.

The Native bearers came rushing anxiously back towards them; terrified and blubbering senseless sounds and shouts.

106

* * * * * * *

"What the hell?" Vern cursed, leaping to his feet.

"Be careful!" Carver warned, stepping up beside him.

Ruby held back, loosening the small .38 revolver strapped to her narrow waist. She wasn't taking any chances with anybody—Vern, Carver, the bearers, or whatever mysterious force that had suddenly attacked them from out of nowhere. Her thoughts blurred. Her senses grew sharp—strange. It seemed like she'd stepped into some kind of a distant past that should have been dead and buried thousands of years before. Now she found herself immersed in this world with a deadly menace that struck without warning or emotion.

A shudder ran through her voluptuous form.

"What the damn hell happened to Johnston?" Vern demanded, not moving forward, but standing frozen and shaken.

"Damned, if I know!" Carver told him.

"You damn cowards!" Ruby shouted, moving forward. "What's wrong with you?"

She moved forward, but when she was opposite the two men, Vern held out an arm, holding her back.

"Stay where you are!" he demanded. For a moment he hesitated nervously; then gripping his gun tighter, he moved forward, cocking the revolver.

"Be careful," Carver told him, shifting his position more solidly next to Ruby.

Step by step Vern spanned the few feet separating him from the large wall which was blocking the thick undergrowth. Finally he came to the place where Johnston had disappeared. There was a large metal door before him. Cautiously, he touched it with the tip of his revolver.

Nothing happened.

"It looks safe to me!" he told the other two, standing and motioning them to his side. "But I don't see...how he—where he went. There's some kind of plate under it. I mean where he disappeared..."

Ruby moved forward and stood beside him. She felt a hard lump in her throat. "Knock on it—maybe he's down there—alive...maybe he'll hear you."

Carver laughed. "I knew she had a brain somewhere," he cried.

"Oh shut up!" Ruby snapped.

Vern tapped the metal lightly.

"Harder!" she told him.

"Take it easy—I don't want to set anything off...we don't know what the hell kind of trap this might be!" Vern tapped louder.

There wasn't any sound from below. He tapped harder.

Nothing.

"Now what?" Carver demanded, rubbing his thick beard.

Vern stood and looked at the door that faced them. "I don't know—really. I'm 'fraid of that damn thing!"

"There must be a way in!"

Just then the door started to open.

There was a scream of terror from the Indian bearers behind them.

Ruby turned just in time to see the bearers dropping their bundles and rushing off into the jungle.

* * * * * * *

When Johnston felt himself land and then fall forward, he forced the action and rolled completely over, springing quickly back to his feet.

After a frantic moment, while he desperately sought to catch his breath, his eyes attempted to focus in the darkness.

It was impossible.

A nervous grind was twisting fearfully in his gut as he searched for his small pocket flashlight. Finally it came out and one flick of his hand brought a dim glow to the blackness.

Hesitantly he examined his surroundings. It took only one moment to see that this was some kind of dungeon trap. Several white skeletons were scattered along the floor, some only half remaining. A shudder ran through him as he realized how deadly a place this must have once been.

Much to his surprise it wasn't a dead end or sealed room, but led to a hallway and deeply worn stone stairway.

Taking a tighter grip on his rifle, he moved slowly forward. He wasn't really too afraid of an attack by man or beasts, but the weapon in his hand gave him a certain amount of security against the unknown.

He moved close to the walls, examining them carefully by the dim light. They were decorated with numerous patterns and pictures, laced and interlaced with aged spider webs. Yet the colors and lines of the pictures seemed as bright and new as if they had been painted yesterday! For some reason the dust had only collected on the naked walls, but not on the actual outlines of the pictures.

It was alien and terrifying.

A shudder of dread passed across his body, but he kept moving forward, up the steps and around the curve that they made at the top.

Then he stopped suddenly, shocked and stunned beyond belief.

Before him was a huge room. On a wall, in its bracket was a torch. Testingly, he reached for it, almost afraid it would crumble at his touch. Surprisingly it was solid and made of a substance unknown to him. Quickly examining it with his lighter, he discovered a small latch that easily slipped downwards.

The top of the torch suddenly became bright lighting the room with a warm glow.

The whole room, walls and floor and ceiling, were golden, the walls patterned with delicate and complicated engravings, colored and lined with brightly rich tones. On the floor were lacy designs made of gems of all colors.

For a moment he was frozen by the splendor. And then he heard the tapping sound from the left of him.

Looking in that direction he was surprised to see a large door that appeared to be of the same design as the one that had been blocking the pathway outside.

Quickly he moved to it and, taking up the huge latch that held it in place, he lifted. Surprisingly it opened with little effort on his part.

Standing before him were Carver, Vern, and

Ruby, white faced and tense with shock.

"I thought you were dead!" Ruby shouted in shocked surprise.

"How'd you get here?" Yates demanded.

Johnston quickly explained and then motioned the others in.

They hesitated, and then Carver suggested: "Let's wait for the others...let them set off all the other traps.

Vern paused and turned. "That's a good idea—"

"It seems to be safe inside," Johnston told them. "We're probably safer there than outside. They must have set up the traps for outsiders—they surely wouldn't for themselves inside."

Yates thought that over for a moment and then nodded. "Okay—but we touch nothing. Nothing at all! Be careful and wait for the Henderson crowd."

They nodded to each other, grinning slightly, and then stepped into the temple.

LOST CITY OF THE DAMNED, BY CHARLES NUETZEL

CHAPTER THIRTEEN

"What, the hell, are they saying?" Dave demanded as Henderson stopped one of the Indian bearers who had suddenly rushed at them from the thick underbrush and game trail.

Henderson shook his head and then started talking to the frightened man in sign language. After a moment of frantic finger and arm and facial movements he turned and looked at Dave. *"They've found the city!"*

"What, the hell?"

"But much more. Two men were killed and one disappeared...then something about an opening door...or something. That's when they ran away!"

"Let's get going!" Dave urged, starting anxiously forward.

"Hold on, we have to be careful," Henderson told him, starting to take the lead.

"I'm familiar with primitive traps and things like that—" His voice faded out, and he started moving forward.

It was ten minutes before they reached the end of the game trail and the large, beautifully carved doorway and wall.

Dave noticed the dead forms of the two Indian bearers. Henderson, at the same time, pointed them out. "Those are the two men he told me about.

113

Watch out for an ambush."

"They must be inside," Henderson told them.

"How'd they get in?" Charlie Quinn asked, looking eagerly at the door.

"That's a good question," Henderson announced, starting to move carefully forward. He reached the door and started exploring its surface delicately with his fingertips. "Watch what I'm doing," he told the others, his voice tense with concentration.

"If anything happens to me—I want you to know what set it off—"

"How do you know that they're inside?" Jean wanted to know, stepping to Dave's side.

"The man I was questioning said something about a door opening—that would have to be this...and it's the logical place for them to be."

His hands were moving along the outer surface of the door when it suddenly opened outwards. A sign of relief passed his lips as he stepped backwards. In his excitement his arm brushed a protruding panel design and the ground below his feet suddenly opened. He disappeared without a word and then the clank of metal hitting metal sounded as the black opening closed again.

Only the huge door beckoned them into the darkness beyond.

They hardly noticed the yell of terror and fear behind them. They didn't notice that the bearers suddenly threw down their bundles, turned and ran back along the path that led out of the valley.

The only thing that Dave, Charlie and Jean were aware of was that Henderson had abruptly vanished—*and the temple door lay open and ready for them to enter...*

* * * * * * *

Jean cried out, her hand going to her mouth and her face becoming white and chilled. "Dad!"

Where had Henderson gone? Was he dead? Injured?

All of them stood paralyzed in shock and it was several minutes before anybody moved. It was Quinn who broke the silence.

"Grab these flashlights—and let's get inside!" he ordered. He passed one to Jean, who took it mechanically, and then one to Dave.

By now Dave was out of his shocked state, and once more his mind was beginning to work swiftly, covering the events of the last couple of minutes. There wasn't anything they could do about Dr. Henderson, not at this moment, anyway. Nothing was left but to go forward and hope for the best.

Leveling his gun, he motioned the others to follow him, and then after clicking his flashlight on he stepped into the darkened chamber before him.

"Be careful," he told them, moving into the center of the room and flashing his light from side to side. An awkward and heavy silence numbed them while they examined the intricate patterns and designs on the walls.

"Look at that!" Charlie exclaimed after awhile. "Well I'll be damned!"

"How beautiful," Jean sighed, her voice breathless.

There was the sound of footsteps, careful and hesitant.

Dave turned toward the sound, flashing his light in that direction, not knowing what to expect. He felt his guts tighten as he saw a shadowy form. Then he recognized the shape as it came into the brighter field of his light.

"Doctor Henderson!" he cried, startled to see the scientist. He had feared they wouldn't see the man.

"Hello—I'm quite all right. Just a bit shaken. The thing I fell through led to a dungeon—no doubt, at one time it was thick with warriors ready to kill anything that fell into it—there's a passageway which leads into..." His voice stopped abruptly as he noticed his surroundings.

"Flash a light on that wall!" he ordered in a tight voice. "Quick!"

He moved to the nearest wall and started looking at it carefully. His eyes were only inches from the marvelous engravings. "Just like—like the one in Africa! It's incredible—really...hard to believe—so hard to believe." His fingers were feeling the surface, trembling slightly. "So much like the—"

"You forget, Doctor," Dave pointed out, "that there are others apparently in this—temple!"

Henderson stiffened. "God—you're right!"

Everybody turned his attention to searching for another doorway out of the chamber. There were two. Dave pointed to the left one and turned to Quinn. "You and Dr. Henderson take that one—Jean and I will go this way."

The other nodded.

"Be careful," Henderson told them. "Maybe Jean should stay—"

"I want to go!"

"All right, all right—" the scientist said, irri-

116

tated, the expression on his face showing how well he knew his daughter's stubborn side. "Suppose that's best, anyway."

Dave stepped toward the doorway.

"Be careful for booby traps, Davy-boy!" Charlie called.

Jean said: "I know something about those things. Dad exposed me to a lot of information...and...just be careful!"

Slowly Dave inched his way forward. Along both walls he could make out the detailed carvings which must, he felt, be relating the history or religious beliefs of the once advanced civilization that had built this temple. The images were blurred in his mind, stretching out to reveal twisting streets, people in strange garments all traveling along pebbled walkways. Golden images were splattered with jewels to brightly tease the mind; set in odd patterns. He couldn't help but marvel at the rich array of valuable stones that were displayed at every turn along the passageway. Mentally, it was impossible to process all the material. And the swift speed in which they were moving made it even more difficult to lock those images into lasting pictures. It was more like watching an ever-changing pattern, dizzily flashing through his consciousness. But nothing was branded there. A flashing pattern mixed with countless gems.

"It's amazing," Jean said in a low, awed voice. "There's no dust or weathering on the colors—notice that?"

"I'd been wondering—it's as if somebody had been keeping it dusted all these centuries."

"Or they are...affixed with some chemical that

resists...it's impossible!" she stated in an awed voice.

There was a turn in the corridor and suddenly Dave found himself in a large room.

A harsh voice sounding at his right startled him. "Okay—*drop it!*"

He turned to look into the bearded face. The man was holding a gun, pointing it directly at the two of them.

Dave's first reaction was to turn and fire his own gun—it was an insane, instinctive response to the unexpected. The second reaction was to drop his gun. But his fingers remained tight.

Just then the room flooded with light, and in the center of it stood two other men, guns leveled at him and Jean. At the same time he saw the voluptuous woman standing in the background; it was impossible to keep from reacting to her striking sexual appeal.

"Drop it!" a tall man in European clothing demanded, motioning with his rifle.

Helpless, Dave let his fingers relax on his gun, and it fell with a clatter to the floor.

* * * * * * *

It had been several hours since the four other explorers had surprised Dave. In the meantime they had bound him and Jean and Charlie. Then the man named Vern Yates ordered Johnston to go with him, and the two of them started down the corridor toward the main entrance.

"They'll find the Doctor!" Carver grinned, rubbing his beard nervously. "Then things will be better!"

'What are you getting at?" Dave demanded, finding it hard to keep his eyes off Ruby. She was one of the most sexually attractive women he had ever seen—even next to Jean she was something else: raw, wanton sex. There was a great difference between the two women. Jean was wholesome, and Ruby, down right erotic. Jean was a woman a man might marry—Ruby was only good for a hungry snack.

"We'll get the Doctor and maybe he can explain a few things that we've found out about this place."

"What have you discovered?" Dave asked. He couldn't feel that all was lost—not as long as Doctor Henderson had something that these others wanted.

"You'll find out soon enough—soon enough...but too late for you!" Carver laughed loudly.

"Stop that!" Ruby ordered in an irritated voice. Her eyes flashed in Dave's direction, and the way they swept his body it wasn't difficult to imagine what she was thinking.

Carver turned savagely toward the woman, snapped angrily: "You ain't telling me where to shut off!"

"Oh, go to hell!"

Carver took a heated step in her direction.

"You better cool down, Captain-man," she told him. "Vern would kill you if you lay one hand on me!"

"Cram that crap down your throat!" Carver snarled, coming to a dead stop. "Vern don't give a living damn about you!"

Ruby's face flushed and then her jaw tightened

and her fingers knotted into small fists. "You better not bet on that!"

The man just laughed tauntingly, but he didn't move closer to her. Instead he turned toward Dave and stepped over to him. "What're you looking at, mister?"

"A goddamned no good son of a bastard who doesn't know how to treat a lady!" Dave spat.

Carver's face hardened and he swung a vicious kick at Dave. The impact of the man's pointed boot jabbed into his thigh painfully, but he refused to react outwardly to the insult.

"Keep your damned trap clamped!" Carver ordered, stepping away and settling down in the far corner.

Ruby was smiling at Dave. She had poised herself in such a way as to show off her figure to the best advantage to his line of vision.

"You're quite a nice little gentleman," she said in a low, sexy voice. "Now, aren't you?"

Dave looked in the woman's direction. He didn't say anything, but his eyes met hers for a long moment. She smiled and then parted her lips and moistened them with her tongue. It was wanton tease, raw flirtation, bold mockery.

He couldn't tame the animal desire flooding up into his body. She was just about the sexiest thing he had ever seen. Pure outright savage lusts on basic drive. The hunger that had been building in him for Jean was suddenly being transferred toward this sexual body. Instinctively he knew she wouldn't hesitate to take him on if given half a chance.

Just then footsteps sounded and Henderson and Charlie Quinn appeared at the entranceway, fol-

120

lowed by Yates and Johnston.

"Okay, move on over there!" Yates ordered. "And don't try anything!"

"They got you, too!" Henderson cried in alarm, his eyes searching his daughter. "Are you all right?"

She nodded silently.

"Shut up—and listen to me!" Yates ordered, regarding Henderson with his rifle. "I got important business to talk over with you!"

"You have nothing of the kind—release those two!" the Doctor ordered.

Yates laughed for a brief moment and then his eyes narrowed and the expression on his face became deadly serious. "You aren't in any position to argue, Doc. We got all the cards on our side—and the only thing you can do is cooperate with us."

"What happens if I don't?"

Yates didn't say anything. Instead he moved toward Jean and placed the barrel of his gun at her throat. He turned and looked meaningfully at her father. "Does that explain things?"

"What happens if I do help? You'll let us go?"

"Now, Doctor—you wouldn't believe me even if I promised. Let's say, from your viewpoint, that you have possibly everything to gain by helping us and everything to lose by refusing to help!" Yates grinned nastily. "So, you figure it out!"

Lost City of the Damned, by Charles Nuetzel

CHAPTER FOURTEEN

Once it was evident that cooperation was the best bet, Dr. Henderson let himself be lead out of the room by Johnston, and immediately went to work, moving across the room to where a huge metal door stood waiting at the end of the chamber.

"I suspect," he said, "this will take us to the central area."

"The treasure?" Johnston wanted to know.

"I assume so," was the doctor's thoughtful reply. "But we have to be careful."

"Be careful then. But get on with it!" Johnston demanded, nastily. "Or else!"

This was surely the end of their long journey. Assuming the door lead to where undiscovered treasures could be found.

"Come on, doc! Get with it!" Johnston demanded, poking the scientist with his pistol.

"That'll get you nowhere. I can't push it too fast!" the man answered, turning his attention to the large metal door standing between them and the unknown. "One mistake and we could be killed!"

Now the difficulty was discovering a way through the door—without setting off any booby traps.

Dave, Jean and Charlie were under the watchful eye of Ruby, a gun in her hand pointed in their direction.

"Can it be done?" Dave heard Johnston demanding of the Doctor, in the other room beyond.

"I don't know—hard to tell...I'll—let me exam-
ine it."

Yates' stood at the entrance, staring into the
room where the scientist was carefully examining
the door.

After a few moments of silence there was a sigh
and then the sound of metal scraping on stone.

"The Doc did it!" sounded Johnston.

Yates moved to join the man.

"God! Almighty!" he shouted.

"It's wonderful!" Henderson's awed voice
sounded.

Dave looked helplessly at Jean and then at Ruby
who was nervously looking in the direction of the
other room. Then she moved to a position where she
could see in. Her jaw dropped in shock.

"What is it?" Dave demanded.

"Fantastic" was her only word.

"Yates, we're going to need help on this—all
the help possible. This can't be handled—"

"Oh, shut up!"

"What are you going to do with us?" Henderson
demanded.

Carver answered: "I don't know, Doc. I really
don't..."

Vern Yates appeared in the room, untied
Charles Quinn. "Untie the others! But if any of you
do anything smart, you're dead! Believe me!"

A few moments later, Dave was standing beside
Jean. And after seeing that she was unharmed, he
took hold of her arm and the two of them moved

toward the doorway and into the other small anti-room. It led on into the large chamber that had just been opened by Doctor Henderson.

All the breath snapped out of him.

Standing in the middle of the huge chamber was a large twenty-foot idol. Green and shiny; inlaid with gems of all kinds and sizes—carved and etched with intricate patterns of gold and silver.

But all this didn't mean anything compared to the horrid and evil looking half-animal, half-human creature in whose shape the idol was patterned.

A god of the lost race.

He didn't even try to understand or explain it. Reality faced them like hard ice. It was there; real; stunning.

Its face was furious with hate. It looked down at them as if actually seeing that they existed. It seemed to have a life of its own—almost breathing out a raging revenge against these intruders of its privacy.

An ancient idol and god of the lost race of—what?

"Doctor—what does it mean?" Dave asked in a hesitant voice, almost afraid to call down the wrath of this hateful image.

"God—idol—call it what you want..." the Doctor's voice told them "What a find—with this—what a find..."

Henderson moved toward the idol, wanting to get a better look at it.

"Stop!" Dave shouted. "You don't know if it's booby trapped or not!"

Henderson paused and turned. "Thanks—I almost forgot!"

125

"Well I'm not afraid!" Carver announced, boldly stepping forward to the base of the idol where there was a small disk on which lay several golden objects that some long dead hand had placed there.

He moved up to the disk and then eagerly reached for one of the objects. "What beauty—wealth...They're made of solid gold—diamonds, rubies..."

That's as far as his voice got.

The air itself seemed to shift, sizzling with flickering light, golden light welled into being, patterns and shapes formed around the huge idol, an image softly formed about it, stretching outwards like a transparent picture of a huge ancient city. A boldly lined street ran down the golden structures. It was illusion, for sure, but very vivid. A very real illusion.

All of them in the chamber gasped in stunned surprise.

"Can you see that?" Charlie cried.

"Christ!" Rita exploded.

It all happened as if some inner switch had been flipped and some three-dimensional image was projected into the room.

A beautifully structure temple lifted up within the city, which stretched between them and the huge green alien figure filling the room so magnificently. The image dominated everything like some supernatural force. What ancient science would have created such an illusion? Vision? Projection?

There was a cracking sound in the air and then one of the huge eyes of the idol shifted in its socket and looked down at Carver. A thin beam of light shot toward the unexpecting man.

One second Carver was touching the small golden figure which held his greedy attention and then the next moment he had stopped existing.

It took several minutes for anyone to actually react to that unexpected and deadly attack. The moment Carver disintegrated before their very eyes, the idol shifted its gaze back to the original position.

The shimmering image of that ancient city flickered away. Darkness filled the room.

Whatever had caused it to take place, it was hard reality. The man had been flashed away to nothingness. That was real enough to crush any doubts anybody in the room might have held.

Everybody was motionless, locked in total shock. It was impossible to believe what had just taken place. The implications were fantastic, unbelievable. No modern scientist could have invented such an illusion as they had witnessed.

The fright-flight impulse was raging, but wouldn't drive them from their frozen position in the room. They were chained in place, gripped by stunned terror and disbelief

Dave was the first to see the possibilities that the unexpected attack from the unknown presented. Everybody seemed paralyzed in place. All Dave and Charlie and Henderson had to do was suddenly jump their three remaining captors.

Without thinking or allowing himself to consider the dangers, he leaped for Vern Yates who was standing open-mouthed and white-faced, looking terrified at the gigantic idol.

"What the—" the man yelled, shocked by the abrupt attack.

Dave grabbed hold of his shoulder, swinging him around and at the same time aiming a hard fist at the man's jaw.

The connection was perfect, and as Yates looked numbly at him, he yanked the man's rifle from his frozen grasp.

Dave heard a shout of alarm to his left and a light scream to his right. Then the sound of a gun shot.

Quickly turning, Dave took in the scene with one sweep of his eyes. A satisfied grin spread across his face.

"It looks like things have changed a bit," he announced in a tight voice.

Henderson had taken Ruby's gun away from her and Charlie had made quick work of Johnston, who now lay on the floor, rubbing his jaw. Yates was lying on his back, out cold.

Dave said to his companions: "I was afraid you guys wouldn't take my cue."

"Buddy—you don't need to ask twice and you ought to know that," Charlie Quinn exclaimed.

"You bastards!" Ruby screamed insanely, her face distorted. "What are you going to do with us?"

"Just keep away from that thing over there!" He pointed to the idol.

"I ain't goin' no way near it!" Charlie announced. "No way!"

Ruby said, again: "What're you planning to do with us?"

Dave thought that over carefully. If they didn't take too many chances and not allow themselves to be caught unawares, there really wasn't any reason to tie up the woman—but the two men were another matter. "Better bundle the two men up—you, Ruby, can stay free if you don't try anything funny!"

A few minutes later his commands had been followed. Then they carefully stepped out of the Chamber of the Green Idol. For some reason they had managed to remain coolly unaware of the danger of another unexpected attack from the eye-ray. It was a simple matter of not touching anything in the chamber. But once alone with Henderson, in the small anti-chamber leading to that of the idol's, Dave turned to the scientist.

"What do you make of it?" he questioned, for the first time beginning to see the implication that the death-ray created. "That...image it showed us!"

Henderson shrugged that away, shook his head from side to side. "It's hard to tell. What ever we saw was illusion...some kind of image projection. Amazing. But never mind that."

It was Ruby who asked, in a surprisingly friendly voice: "What does it mean, Doc?"

Henderson glanced at the women, then said: "Who knows. But that's not the danger...just an image. How it was triggered, what kind of advanced science might have made it...I won't even try to guess. Right now we have other issues to deal with!"

"Yeah, I bet," Ruby snapped. "How to get the treasures out of here..."

Henderson shrugged that off.

Carol said: "There's more here than treasures!"

"Tell me, girl!" Ruby snapped. "We came for gold!"

Dave noted: "Well you're out of the action right now, babe!"

"Don't bet your life on that!"

Charlie Quinn suggested: "Maybe we should tie her up, too!"

"No. Not yet, if she promises to be…"

"I promise," Ruby stated in a very serious voice. "I'll not do anything…" The last sounded somewhat alarmed and frightened as her eyes glanced back towards the other room. "What's going to happen now?"

Henderson offered: "No doubt the idol is set up only to protect its possessions—anyone who tries to steal from it. But how, I don't know—it's out of my field of knowledge. Nor is it my prime concern."

Ruby exploded: "What else matters? Didn't you come for the … treasures?"

Carol snapped: "What treasures? The gold? Jewels? Or ancient ruins? There are treasures here you can't imagine. Only a fool would be thinking only about money. This is a scientific expedition!"

Dave glanced at her, felt a pang of guilt. For him the whole trip had basically started out as nothing but a treasure hunt. Now he didn't know. He turned to the doctor, said: "You must have run into something like it in Africa—"

"Not quite—you have to understand that it was a much smaller place—just one room—unless there were underground chambers that we didn't have a chance to explore...we were interrupted by the natives before we had any chance to really investigate anything to a scientific way."

"What kind of people could have built all this?"

Henderson's eyebrows raised helplessly. "That's a question I don't believe we'll ever know. Maybe I'll find some information by looking around in the room. The main thing, I take it, is to keep from touching anything."

"What about the pit you fell into—"

"I accidentally brushed some part of the protruding design of the wall. Places like this, many times, were booby trapped in order to protect the sacred grounds for only those who were running things at the time."

The Doctor had become highly nervous at this point of the conversation. "I'm anxious to see things right now—" he said, looking toward the larger Idol Chamber. "The sooner I start nosing around the better."

Those were his last words before turning and suddenly walking into the other room.

"Doctor!" Dave called, "For God's sake—be careful!"

* * * * * * *

Henderson wouldn't, at first, let anybody else enter the room, outside of himself, for fear that they might set off some other deathly rays or traps. He was looking for signs of a doorway or entrance to the Idol or behind the Idol, to another room. But there wasn't any that Henderson could find. It was tiresome work, and Charlie, Jean, and Dave took turns watching the prisoners.

It was on Dave's watch that Ruby started making her first play.

Henderson was tirelessly looking through the Idol Chamber. Jean had gone in and convinced her father that she would be of help to him, and Charlie was resting in the anti-chamber. Ruby and Dave were in the corridor outside the large room in which

LOST CITY OF THE DAMNED, BY CHARLES NUETZEL

the two groups had first met each other.

Dave was finding it hard to keep his eyes off the quite stunning Ruby. She was leaning on the other wall just a few feet from him. The way she was posed seemed pointedly sensual. She kept looking at him with a peculiar expression on her face.

"What are you with these jerks for?" she demanded, staring directly into his eyes.

He shook himself and puffed lightly on his cigarette. "They aren't jerks, lady!"

"You know what I mean—scientists...no money in that! And you have the look of a man hungry for money—a lot of it!"

Dave smiled broadly, and let a shrug be his answer.

"Can I have one?" she asked, indicating the cigarette he was smoking, thus changing the subject. She leaned closer to him as he lit a cigarette for her.

"You look like a pretty right guy..." She smiled invitingly. "I appreciate you deciding to trust me."

"Well, hardly, but..."

"You know what I mean. Not binding me up like a tossed pig! Like you did the men." She took a deep drag on the cigarette, all the time her eyes watching his. "What makes you think I not as dangerous at they are?"

"I suppose I don't," he admitted.

"Well...thanks again. Nice of you. Nice to be trusted ...kinda trusted that is." She winked and smiled rather wantonly, her eyes drifting over his solid frame. "Makes a woman think...there's a chance for her. With a man like you."

The abrupt and unreasonable change in her mood left him somewhat startled, even breathless.

Her eyes were now looking deep into his, and the sparkle they projected left nothing to the imagination as to what she was thinking. The woman was literally raping him in her mind.

And he couldn't get his eyes off her. He tried, but found himself frozen with fascination.

"What I mean is..." she continued, leaning closer, her face now only inches away, "if somebody was to help me—you know what I mean...Well, I'd do *anything!*"

She was so close now that it would have been so easy to kiss her. "You know I can be pretty nice to a man. When I want to be."

The scent of her heated body and the trembling nearness of her lips were torrid temptation almost impossible to resist. Ruby was the kind of woman a man used and enjoyed—the kind of woman who quite obviously enjoyed sex with no holds barred.

Suddenly she surged forward, melting into his arms with a heavy sigh of relief. Dave wasn't even sure he'd done anything but stand there—yet his arms were around her. They had moved automatically in response to her warm lips coming in contact with his. Her body surged hungrily against him.

Just then Jean walked in on them.

The silence was numbing. He felt his insides go cold as he saw the startled and hurt expression in her eyes. Her face went white, but her lips were set.

"Dad found the opening to the Idol!" she announced in a loud voice.

Dave stepped away from Ruby, truly concerned about Jean's reaction to what she'd just seen. It took a few moments before her words sank in.

Then he noted that Charlie Quinn was standing

at the entrance, silently watching everything. How long he'd been there was impossible to guess. The expression his face revealed just how correctly he'd sized things up.

Jean glanced angrily at Ruby, but she said nothing to the woman.

Instead she made an unexpectedly decisive move at that point, stepping forward, taking Dave's hand. "Come!"

She led him from the room into the Chamber of the Idol, leaving Charlie and Ruby alone.

CHAPTER FIFTEEN

The minute that Charlie was alone with Ruby he made it a point to notice the huge opening which her now gaping blouse made, half unbuttoned as it was. At first she didn't notice the direction of his stare, but then her eyes met his, and her lips smiled knowingly.

"Like what you see? Want it? Bet you'd be fun!" She mocked him knowingly, quite sure of herself and the man's limited ability to resist. He was an easy mark—not like Dave Sheldon. "Bet you'd like to..."

She was thrusting her breasts forward slightly, actually thrilling to the wild, animal desire bursting in the man's eyes. It was almost comical!

He grinned, savagely feasting on her. From the expression on his face Ruby could see the raw heated desire that took total control of the man's primitively driven mind.

"Wanna play?" she asked, throatily. "I'm not picky. Any good man in a storm!"

Then she added: "And you...look pretty good!"

She laughed deliciously, almost experiencing an orgasm at the man's reaction. His eyes couldn't get off her body.

"And I bet you're a really good man, once you start on a woman!" She could almost laugh at the situation. He was a joke; but just the kind she needed at that moment. And Ruby knew exactly how to drive a man beyond his limits of resistance. Playing Charlie Quinn was a child's game.

Charlie's face smiled broadly. "Baby—you're my..."

He stopped suddenly.

For in one swift move she jerked off her blouse. A thrilling stab of excitement moved through her as she watched his eyes visually devouring her voluptuous breasts.

Charlie didn't need any encouragement. He grabbed eagerly for Ruby, drawing her body close to his.

Suddenly she felt the hard metal under her fingers and then without any warning she pulled the man's gun from its holster and rammed it into Quinn's stomach.

He almost doubled over in pain from the impact of the barrel in his guts. "What, the hell?"

"A little surprise for you, lover," she told him, stepping back, while keeping the gun level with his stomach. "Make one false move and you'll find yourself dead!"

She motioned him to where Yates and Johnston were tied and gagged in the other room. "Okay, let them loose!" she demanded.

Quinn did what she told him to do, without a word. A moment later the two men were standing, rubbing circulation into their arms and legs. Ruby quickly gathered a couple of rifles from the corner and handed them to her two companions.

Yates checked over his weapon and then grunted.

"Come on, let's go get the others," he said, jabbing his rifle into Charlie's back.

* * * * * * *

As Dave went with Jean into the Chamber of the Idol, he heard Henderson's voice from behind the idol, "over here."

A few moments later, Dave was looking at an opening in the huge statue's back; it led down a stone staircase sharply dipping into the blackness. Henderson stood at the stairway holding one of the mysterious torches they'd discovered which lighted everything around them so brightly.

"I waited until you could get here—I don't think it's a good idea for me—or anybody, for that matter—to wander around by themselves..." The scientist's voice faded out as if his mind became interested in something other than what he was talking about. He turned silently, motioning them to follow.

Dave needed no second invitation.

Jean moved between him and her father, carefully making her way downwards.

"How'd you find your way into the idol?" Dave asked.

"Accidentally, really. I'm not quite sure how it happened. I was concentrating on a particular set of symbols that puzzled me. I must have triggered the mechanism when one of the design patterns moved and then the door slid open."

They were walking down the deep, narrow passageway when it came to an abrupt end. Dave was unaware of it and bumped right into Jean, almost knocking her over. But the contact was electric. It seemed like his every nerve stood up at attention. The same it happened several times before—but this time it was even stronger, shockingly exciting, as if that one embrace with Ruby had put his whole nervous system on edge, and all it took was this one brushing contact to fire it up again.

Jean turned toward him, an irritated remark starting to push past her teeth, but the expression in her eyes reflected the heated desire reacting in her body. Physically, this was the right moment to take her in his arms—they both wanted it—even though it was the wrong time and place.

"Just a moment," Henderson told them, starting to explore the outer rim of the door. "This must work much like the other doors."

"Be careful," Jean warned, in a slightly shaky voice.

The door smoothly slid open and Henderson moved forward into a small room.

Jean and Dave followed.

At that moment they heard, far above them, the sliding of a door. Dave started and Henderson turned.

"What was that?" Jean asked.

The scientist looked worried. "I don't know!"

At the same moment the door they had just stepped through slid shut.

Henderson rushed toward it, but it was sealed tight. After a frantic moment he turned.

"We're trapped—" then his voice faded and his face became white and ashen.

"God! God almighty!" He was looking beyond Dave and Jean.

Dave turned, and the instant he saw what Henderson was looking at, he felt his insides twist horribly.

Lining the wall was one mass of levers, made of solid golden metal. Centering in the wall was a large opening like mirror that looked out into the room.

But far more shocking than all this was the scene which was taking place outside the mirror. They saw Yates, Johnston, Ruby and Quinn walking into the room.

Henderson smiled sardonically, and moved to the front of the panel where all the levers were located beside the transparent section of the wall.

Henderson started to reach for a lever.

"Be careful—don't fool around!" Dave yelled.

"I am—being careful..." Cautiously, the scientist started examining the switches.

"It's a shame that we can't give them a little scare," Jean said, leaning closer over her father's shoulder.

Henderson chucked. "That's not what I'm looking for—but it's a good idea. What I want is the master switch, though, which will shut this idol off. I'll have to find the switch which opens the doors too...but maybe we'll have a little fun in the meantime..."

"Ah—now I see...this controls the eye—that there..." the scientist indicated the small gem at the side of the lever, "no doubt activates the ray—let's find out!"

He pressed the gem and a thin beam shot outwards, exploding a huge hole into the ceiling. Chuckling he started flicking switches and hitting buttons.

"What a civilization this must have been—

advancement beyond our wildest dreams!" He was like a child with a new toy.

Suddenly the door behind them opened.

"Stop!" Dave cried, who had been keeping his eye on the barrier that held them captive.

There was the sound of another door sliding. "The one on top must have opened, too!" he announced, placing a hand on Henderson's shoulder. "Come on—let's get out of here!"

"No—wait! I want to find the lever which will cut this damn thing off!"

A sigh of hopeful surprise sounded as his hand flipped across a new gem.

"I think I found it, at last!"

"Okay…. Let's get out of here! And fast!" Dave took hold of Jean's hand and the contact was electric. But he forced himself to ignore the ecstatic excitement that jerked through his whole body. He started pulling her after him, quickly moving up the corridor and then out of the Idol, around it and then out of the Chamber and toward the outside, forgetting all about the other group.

He was in the huge entrance chamber that led to the outside world when he was brought to a sudden stop by a gruff voice.

"Just stay where you are," Vern Yates demanded.

"Don't move—*or you're dead!*"

There was a distant rumble from the ground underneath them. And then the floor shook slightly.

Just then Henderson came walking out.

"We better get out of here," he announced. "Cutting off that Idol must have started some self-destructive mechanism—that would explain the..."

140

His voice trailed off as he noticed Yates, Johnston and Ruby holding guns on the rest of them.

"So that explains it," Yates said, smiling.

"What?" Ruby wanted to know.

"They turned the machine off!" Charlie Quinn announced, blurting the words out before he had thought it over.

Johnston smiled greedily. "Well, well—how nice. Now, maybe we can stash away a few of those little old statues...so nice of you, Doctor!"

Lost City of the Damned, by Charles Nuetzel

CHAPTER SIXTEEN

"You don't understand," Henderson objected, frantically. "When I turned off that machine." Another rumbling in the ground beneath them interrupted his voice. "See what I mean?"

"What?" Vern demanded, sneeringly.

"That rumbling—the idol must have been connected with some self-destructive..."

The floor shook violently then.

"We've got to get out of here!" Henderson told the others. "This place might come tumbling down upon us any moment!"

"Oh shut up, you old fool!" Johnston ordered: "Let's get going!"

"What are you going to do?" Jean asked, alarmed.

"Take a handful of those statues. They're worth a fortune!"

"We can't go back in there! Everything is already starting to crumble," Henderson objected.

Dave felt a shudder run through him. He wanted to run from the place. Then suddenly his mind seemed to cloud slightly. Blackness moved across his vision and suddenly he felt himself being raised—as if somebody had lifted him. He realized it was only an illusion. Then his eyes opened or cleared—he didn't know which—and he found himself looking at an alien landscape. It was only for a moment. And in that moment he recognized the valley where they had come to reach this temple. But it was different. Virgin. New. Fields stretching in all directions. People walking in and out between buildings. It was as if watching a movie, shifting before him. It was slightly distorted with fuzziness, and before he could focus on anything, it jerked into nothingness. For a moment he thought he had been seeing things—that his mind was cracking.

Then the entrance chamber popped back into existence before his eyes. The others around him were standing, glassy-eyed, as if paralyzed. Nobody moved at first, then one by one they shook themselves and looked at each other.

"God, that—what was that?" Johnston cried, his face white.

"Another dream from the past!" Henderson announced in a weak and slightly shaking voice. "A dream projected by some mind-recording mechanism. It probably explains the previous illusion we all saw."

"But how? How?" Quinn demanded in an awed voice.

"Man does not know everything. We have not discovered everything—there are many things, yet, for us to find out—we're still babes in the woods. Who is to say that if some earlier civilization developing in a different direction from our own couldn't have discovered and found out things that we do not, yet, know about. Recording mental images and then projecting them."

"Let's get out of this creepy place," Ruby cried, a shiver running down her body. "Let's get the hell

144

out!"

"We came for something—and damn it all, we're getting it!" Vern told them. "Come on—with me...all of you!"

They all looked in his direction. There wasn't any arguing with a gun.

The floor trembled again. The walls seemed to shake, as another, louder, rumble sounded from beneath them.

"It's dangerous going in there," Henderson cried.

"We came a long way—I want what we came for."

Dave felt a sickening grind inside him. Looking at Jean he realized that there were other things more important than money and fortune. "Let Jean and her father leave, first."

"No'!" Vern told him. "Come on!"

They were forced down the corridor and finally into the room of the Idol. "Take as many of those objects as you can!" Johnston ordered them.

Dave did as Vern ordered, walking up to the disk and reaching for one of the golden statues that were encrusted with priceless jewels. He half expected one of the eyes of the huge green idol to move down toward him—but it didn't.

For a moment it was impossible not to look in awed wonder at the small statue. The carving was perfect—the face of a human, and the body of an ape. Little designs and patterns were intertwined and dotted with red, green, blue, yellow, brown and clear jewels. The value of just that one object would be worth a fortune—take care of a person's financial problems for life.

"Come on—hurry up!" Vern ordered, as the floor started shaking more violently. "We gotta hurry...."

From the gaping hole in the ceiling which Henderson had made with the idol's eye-ray earlier, came a trickling of dirt and dust, and then a few stones clattered to the floor under the opening.

"Hurry—grab what you can!" Johnston cried, rushing forward and taking hold of a small jeweled and carved box. He put it in his pocket and then grabbed several other objects, stuffing them wherever there was a place for them. "Come on—take as many as you can carry."

For the moment nothing seemed important except doing as Johnston told them. Not because the other man held a gun at his back, but because something inside Dave drove out all passion and desire and all interest in anything other than gathering as many of these priceless items as he could hold.

A fever far greater than fear now possessed all of them.

Henderson was at his side, and Charlie and Jean and Vern and Ruby—all eagerly filling their arms and pockets with as many statues and artifacts as they could possibly carry.

The floor was beginning to vibrate more violently and the rumbling that had started underneath them was now beginning to resound on every side as the walls began to shake.

"Let's get out of here!" Charlie Quinn shouted—starting for the door.

Jean and Dave turned with him and started rushing down the corridor, as the walls started to crack.

There was a horrible grating sound. Dirt and

146

dust began to fall all around them. There was a scream from behind them and then they heard Vern's voice crying that they had all better get out.

Dave felt the floor shifting and before they could move much further just in front of him and Jean and behind Quinn the floor started caving in. There was a crashing sound and they found themselves facing a three-foot gap in the floor.

"Jump over it!" Dave told her.

"No—I'm afraid."

"Just step over it—there's nothing to be afraid of!" he urged, pushing her forward. "Quinn—Charlie...give us a hand!" Quinn ignored him, continuing to dash for the entrance chamber.

The walls were violently grating and shifting. Dave stepped over the three-foot hole and then reached for Jean, dropping some of the idols and gems that were in his arms. "Here, take my hand."

Jean leaped the distance and then the two of them rushed onward.

They heard shouts behind them and her father's voice cursing and yelling.

They reached the entrance chamber when suddenly the world seemed to spin violently around them. The floor was heaving upwards, and the ceiling was beginning to crash.

"Come on!" Dave told Jean, who had turned and looked back down the crumbling corridor behind them. "What about Dad?" she cried frantically.

"Get, the hell, out of here!" he told her pushing her forward, toward the entrance.

"But Dad—I can't leave him!" she cried.

"It's everybody for himself!" he told her, pushing her against her will. "I'll go back!"

A gap cracked in the ceiling, and rock and dirt and metal fell downward several feet from them.

"Hurry!" Dave pushed her out of the entrance and then turned and started back across the crumbling room. He saw Henderson and Johnston and Yates and Ruby standing at the edge of the corridor, looking at a monstrous hole blocking their one avenue of escape. The wall suddenly heaved and then crumbled.

"You'll have to jump!" Dave told Henderson, ignoring the rest.

There were four to five feet of black opening between them. It would almost take a running leap, but there wasn't any room or time.

Dave thought desperately about what he could possibly do. Then suddenly another part of the ceiling crashed downwards and a large metal beam fell within a few feet of the gaping hole.

Quickly he reached it and started lifting. It was lighter than he would have imagined and he easily dragged it over to the hole. The beam was only about six inches wide, but at least seven feet long. Hurriedly he slid it across the gap and Johnston and Yates and Ruby pushed their way across, ahead of the scientist, using their guns to hold the older man back.

Then Henderson started carefully to move step by step along the narrow metal walkway. The room was exploding and crumbling around him. The left wall caved in and just as Henderson was at the end of his perilous journey another grating and rumbling sounded and the other side of the hole suddenly erupted, and the metal beam slid out from under him.

Dave desperately reached for the older man and his hand locked on the other's wrist. But too late. The hold wasn't strong enough. The floor shook and part of the ceiling fell with an exploding crash just two feet from him. A jagged chunk of rock jumped up, striking Dave on the side of the head.

Desperately he attempted to keep his balance and at the same time hold onto Henderson. Then he felt a strong arm grab hold of him and he turned slightly to see Charlie Quinn reaching for Henderson's arm. The world shifted again and Dave went spinning backwards.

Quinn was pushed to the edge of the hole and then the ground under him dropped suddenly, the walls started to sway and then fell forward, crashing down upon the two men before Dave could do anything to save either of them.

There wasn't time to think of anything after that except getting out himself before it was too late.

Frantically he got to his feet and started rushing for the entrance that was only about five yards away. His heart sickened as he saw the doorway start to shift, and then the floor in front of it split with a terrible grinding sound. All he could do was jump and hope for the best.

He jumped, without thinking and without looking, desperately fighting to save his life. All the statues and idols had long been forgotten and dropped; it was his life and nothing else that he was interested in now.

It seemed forever before his feet reached the other side of the huge split. It had been well over a five-foot jump.

Just as he landed on the other side and sprang

forward, still being carried by his own momentum, he heard an ear splitting crashing sound!

The world shook and then he found himself being spun forward by the impact of something hitting him on the back of his head.

The universe clouded and started whirling rapidly around him, and blackness began to throb painfully, blanking out all sight and sound and consciousness.

* * * * * * *

When Jean saw Dave fall unconscious to the ground, her heart gave a tight jerk. At first she wasn't even aware that her father hadn't come out with him. Nothing seemed to matter in the least—she couldn't think about anything except the horrifying fact that she'd found a man she could have loved and married and been with for the rest of her life. Now she realized the awful truth about herself—but too late.

Dave Sheldon lay there, blood welling out of the ugly gash at the back of his head. She thought he was dead. In frantic desperation she threw herself down at his side, a sob choking in her throat.

Vern Yates turned toward her with a sneer sounding from his throat. "The slob is dyin'!" he snapped, "Why bother?"

"Come on, let's get out of here!" Ruby cried, tugging on his arm. "We gotta get out of this creepy place."

"Yeah," Johnston agreed, looking greedily down at the armful of gold and jewels in his hands. "Let's get out of here!"

150

He turned away and started walking down the game trail leading out of the valley.

"Come on, you blonde bitch!" Yates told Jean, taking hold of her arm and trying to pull her away from the still body of Dave.

"No—no!" she cried, fighting with him. "He's alive!"

"What the hell do I care?" Yates cursed, struggling with her. "Come on—or we'll leave you!"

"I can't leave him like this—help me...help me pull him away—Jean started pulling on Dave's arm, trying to drag him farther from the exploding temple.

"Leave her with him!" Ruby demanded. "The little whore wants her man—let her die with him!"

Yates stepped away from Jean. He shrugged his shoulders and then turned.

"Let's blow this joint!"

Without another word he walked to Ruby's side and the two of them started off after Johnston, out of the valley.

LOST CITY OF THE DAMNED, BY CHARLES NUETZEL

CHAPTER SEVENTEEN

Dave felt the throbbing pain, first. Then an ebbing light seemed to be dancing before his eyes. He was aware of floating in space and then slowly he seemed to settle downwards and then he became aware of sounds.

Night sounds.

Night jungle sounds.

Still feeling sluggish, he opened his eyes.

Darkness surrounded him. Slowly he became accustomed to the night light.

He was lying on his back, looking up at the sky. Stars were shining brightly and a moon, half-full, was bathing the night with its dim light.

He heard a sound to his left and turned, startled.

"How are you feeling?" Jean's voice asked him.

For a moment he thought he was hearing things, then he saw her shadowy form sitting on the ground next to him.

She leaned over and reached out a delicate hand, caressing his forehead.

"You feel better," she told him in a low voice.

"Your...father..."

She shook her head. "I know," was all she said.

"I tried—"

"I know."

Dave looked around him. They were in a clear-

153

ing about a hundred yards from the crumbled ruins of the temple in the background. There was a large fire just a few feet away from them.

"Where are the others?" he asked, painfully sitting up now.

"They left us."

"What?"

"They left!"

He couldn't believe her words at first. It seemed incredible that anybody human could leave one helpless woman and an unconscious man alone, without weapons or supplies in the jungle.

"Why didn't you go with them?"

She just shrugged her shoulders helplessly and then leaned closer.

"I couldn't leave you—" she said.

"Damn it all!"

Dave tried to stand up. It took effort and he felt his jaw clamping tightly as the ache in his head shot through him. Finally he got to his feet.

"What now?"

He walked over to the fire. The night was cold and his mouth dry.

"Try to get back," she said.

"You should have gone with the others..."

"They'd just—well they would have..."

"You'd have at least had a chance—this way you..."

"This way I have you." The way she said the words made him turn and look hard at her. "It was bad enough losing Dad, but...I lost him many times in the past. And I couldn't lose you, too."

"That's not much!" he said.

"It's all I have—now."

154

He turned toward Jean. She was sitting very close to him, and for the first time he noticed how tired she looked.

"You've had it, haven't you?"

She nodded silently.

Impulsively he placed an arm around her shoulder and drew her nearer to him. The contact was electrically charged, but he held back the desire to crush her to him.

"You—you must have..." He wanted, to say something about her father, but couldn't make himself speak about it—the words, the right words, wouldn't come.

"That temple?" he finally asked.

"Completely destroyed."

"God, what kind of people—civilization."

She turned and looked up at him, her eyes were moist. "I—it was terrible—wasn't it? So terrible. And so much beauty back there crumbling away. We'll never know what it might have meant. Where they came from, what their history was all about...all those people lived their lives—and now the evidence of what they had left behind is...lost."

Her lips were trembling slightly. "It is really so sad."

Tears were ebbing in her eyes. "Poor Dad! All...gone!"

She leaned closer. "I...can't deal with that!'

It took all the control he had in him to keep from kissing her right then.

Instead he gently pulled her closer and comforted her. His arm was around her shoulder and he patted her head tenderly. She was trembling a little. The tears ran down her cheeks.

"I won't cry!" she announced. "Dad would never have wanted that."

"Cry if you want!" he murmured softly.

She shivered, then sobbed, crumbling against him. For a long time neither of them said anything. Her tears faded after a while. Then he was only aware of Jean's breathing against him. He was torn between wanting to comfort her, hold her and, at the same time, make love to her.

"What a horrible place that was..." he offered, brushing her cheek.

"Dad—he thought...maybe it was the interconnection with...Atlantis or something...something even older." She shivered.

"Or something that was—more advanced than our own world—it doesn't seem possible!" he nodded. "Nobody would believe what we witnessed. It is just impossible!"

"Anything—is possible..." She seemed to be half thinking out loud, and the way she said the last words made Dave wonder if maybe she was talking about something other than the civilization or the ancient scientific wonders they had seen.

"Hold me tight!" she sobbed lightly. "Please."

He couldn't refuse that request, even though he knew in advance where it would lead—the only place it *could* lead.

Dave pulled her closer to him and was surprised the way her arms slid around his neck and the eager pressure of her breasts as they crushed against him.

For a long time they held each other, not speaking, not thinking. He wanted to make love to her, and he knew that there *would* be no stopping now. This was the moment, the time, the instant—it

156

would build, and there wasn't anybody to stop them now; there wasn't anybody left to get in their way. And right or wrong, it didn't matter because they might both be dead the next day—and all that counted now was *tonight*—this moment they had together.

He felt her breath getting deeper and heavier. She seemed to move even closer to him and he could feel the beating of her heart.

Without even knowing exactly how it happened he found his lips on her throat, feeling the silky smooth texture, and the light pulse of her under them.

"Love me..." she whispered so softly that he could hardly hear it. "Love me...my love."

He didn't need another word. She wanted him and he wanted her.

Slowly he laid her down on the ground, stretching out against her. For a long moment he looked down at her, deep into her eyes which were moist and eager. Her lips were trembling and open. Her breathing had become short and rapid.

He felt delicate arms slide around his body and pull him tightly against her. Then their lips met, first tenderly, just touching, and then anxiously moist and open and penetrating.

Her tongue searched eagerly, rapidly darting and anxiously making contact with his. Her body moved nervously under him. He felt her legs shift and her whole body surge up against his.

He slid his hand down to her breast and she arched up against his searching fingers. Then frantically he sought to pull aside the cloth. It was only moments before his hands were caressing naked flesh, his lips circled downwards, frantically kissing her soft creamy skin.

The passion swelled up over them, blanketing all thoughts and all awareness of anything except their starved bodies, emotions and souls.

Reality seemed to shift into a series of touches, caresses, sensations that wrapped themselves around both of them, fusing them together in an over-whelming mutual desire that locked them into one total being.

It was wonderful making love to Jean. All the waiting, the tormented days, the frustrated hours and the lonely moments now seemed worth it. She had been worth waiting for! This moment seemed to be an eternity that flung them up to the heavens on a wave of love and ecstasy and affection and wild tenderness. Their universe suddenly dispersed into a billion exploding stars that shot up into space and disappeared from all awareness and knowledge and consciousness.

The world spun around him, clouding in the wonder of Jean's perfect body, united with his. This was more than just passion or lust or sex. It was something that he never thought he could ever feel again after his wife had died. Now he knew that he had found the woman who could mean everything to him. He had found a woman whom he wanted to be with for the rest of his life. And the irony was, this might fairly well be the truth—regardless! Life might be cut short—any moment during the next few days.

It wasn't fair that now, when he had found his new love, this love for Jean, that it should be so short a time— that it should come so late.

158

Too late—much too late, for both of them.

The world slowly ebbed back and he found himself lying exhausted next to her.

He looked down at her and tried to smile. In one way it wasn't so hard. She was lovely and he loved her.

Their lips met heatedly for a moment and he delighted in the wonderful taste and smell and thrill of her.

They had found each other; even if it was too late; and he realized that she was worth dying for—only he didn't like the idea that Jean might have to die, too!

* * * * * * *

Dark faces watched the three whites as they moved through the underbrush. They watched in silence, but waited for the right moment—the time when they arrived at the right place…and then they would attack again!

The three of them were just setting up a fire for the evening camp. It was their second day out from the temple and they were tired and wearied from the long hours of travel and carrying the armloads of artifacts.

Nobody talked much to each other. They each seemed to be in a world of their own—uninterested in the others, and only concerned with their treasures. They only talked when it was necessary.

Ruby couldn't help feeling almost guilty about leaving Jean and Dave behind, helpless and without any food or weapons. But the guilt was half-false. Mostly, it was just a little annoying undercurrent that only dampened her excitement at the wealth she had been able to gather from the temple.

Yates didn't seem to care about anything. His eyes just glowed on the handful of trinkets he'd taken.

Johnston was the only one who was alert to his surroundings.

He had built a fire and was just starting to get things ready for a meal when he was disturbed by a noise in the shrubbery behind him. He turned rapidly, pointing his gun in that direction.

Standing there in the darkness, all but hidden, was a dark face looking at him. In the nose was a white bone, the eyes were white and gleaming. When he saw that he'd been noticed, he stepped boldly forward, extending his spear.

Several others followed his example.

It took Johnston only one moment to access the situation. He didn't wait to think—he only reacted. His hand went quickly toward his hip and in one quick action the gun was gripped tightly in his fingers.

He squeezed and fire exploded from the barrel.

The head-hunter looked shocked and then his face twisted in agony as a reddish hole erupted from his chest. A moment later he was face downwards on the ground.

The others looked startled and a mumble went up amongst them. Johnston fired again and heard shouts of pain and terror sound from another head-hunter somewhere in the jungle thickness.

"What, the hell?" screamed Yates, reaching for his rifle while at the same time dodging a spear which had been thrown at Johnston. His rifle exploded into action just as Ruby took in the situation and pulled the gun from the holster at her side. She fired point blank at one head-hunter smiling almost happily as she saw him spin around and silently slip to the ground, his side a bloody red mass of torn flesh and bone.

The last two remaining head-hunters turned and ran into the jungle in terror.

"We'd better get the hell out of here!" Yates told them "They'll be back...they'll be back in full force, this time!"

They gathered up their treasures and quickly started down the pathway which would take them in the direction of the river and finally to their small yacht.

* * * * * * *

It was pitch black and Ruby was so tired of branches and bushes hitting her face that she felt like screaming. Sweat was rolling down her arms and she could hardly stand the tension of expecting attack from either side and at any moment.

Johnston was behind her and Yates in front.

The moon was hidden behind clouds, and the treetops, interlacing like a high ceiling above them, kept out any possible light from the stars.

The night sounds of the jungle seemed to have abruptly quieted, and the silence weighed heavily on her. She expected a dark face to jump out from behind every tree or bush.

They had been treading through the underbrush for nearly two hours and every muscle in her body was aching. Her mind was dizzy from all the strain.

The only thing that kept her going was the fear for her life and the fortune she had slung over her back in the knapsack. And that was getting heavier and heavier with every step.

"Can't we rest?" Johnston moaned behind her.

"Go ahead—but I'm continuing." Yates whispered back.

"I don't know how much further I can go," Ruby told the other two.

"Just think about that pretty little head of yours separated from your neck—that'll keep you going!" Yates told her.

Just then he came to an abrupt stop. A cry of alarm burst from his lips. Then he whipped around, his eyes wide with terror and his mouth open in pain. A spear was projecting from his stomach. Bloody and jagged. His body was already beginning to fall forward as a cry of pain screamed into the night from his trembling and now red-soaked lips.

Ruby didn't wait to think. Her gun fired twice into the darkness and a moan of agony and the sound of a body hitting the ground rewarded her.

Then she felt strong arms grabbing at her shoulders. She turned and squeezed the trigger of her gun once more, a scream of terror bursting from her lips.

That's when she felt the sharp agonizing burn rip through her guts.

The pain was overwhelming, but she didn't pass out. She just stood there, unable to move. The dreadful pain digging through her every cell. She couldn't even scream out. She was conscious of her finger jerking on the trigger of the pistol in her hand, but there weren't any responding gun shots.

Then she turned, spinning toward the ground,

conscious that life was fading and that there wasn't anything she could do about it. The last thing she was aware of was seeing Johnston's dead body lying on the ground as she fell against it....

* * * * * * *

It was a couple of days before Dave and Jean came upon the bodies of the three head-hunters. The picture was all too clear.

"I'm afraid that our friends didn't get too far from here..." he announced, gathering up a couple of the spears from the head-hunters that were left behind them.

Two hours later they came across three grisly bodies.

They had been walking through the jungle, almost happily content, in love and ready to face any difficulty that might cross their path. Both of them were confident in finding their way back to civilization if they could survive the obvious other dangers of such a journey. And so far they'd been amazingly lucky. They were armed and the distance wouldn't be too far before they would find the yacht that had brought them down the Amazon River. And the further they got away from the ruins the more unbelievable they seemed. Nothing mattered, any more, outside of their newly discovered love for one another. They walked hand in hand, aware of the physical contact, and content.

Then suddenly Dave came to a halt. His insides felt a stab of agonized sickness. Quickly he turned to Jean, to turn her around. But he was too late. Her face was deathly white.

"Oh, God—how...how horrible!" she cried, her voice gagging on the words. She covered her eyes with her hands. "God—oh God!"

In the foliage before them were three headless bodies. Fully clothed.

On the ground next to the bodies were the treasures that had brought all of them to South America to face their fate. Gems and statues and artifacts were scattered, as if they had been examined carelessly and then thrown aside.

It took only a few minutes to gather up some of the scattered treasures and supplies. They took only what they could easily carry. But it was enough to assure a very, very comfortable future for them. They started off toward the Amazon River.

* * * * * * *

A little over a couple of weeks later, Dave was lying on the deck of the large yacht, with Jean next to him.

The sun was hot, but it felt good to him. In fact everything felt good to him, now that they were, at last, safe and together.

He looked across at Jean, half sleeping.

How I love her, he thought, leaning over and kissing her cheek.

She squirmed slightly and looked up.

"Hello, darling," she murmured, contentedly.

He leaned lower and their lips met for a long, passionate kiss.

Just think, he was saying to himself as they tenderly embraced each other, *I had to come all this way to South America, and see the wonders of a lost civilization in order to realize the real treasures in the world.*

He looked down at the greatest treasure in the world: Jean—a woman he loved and who loved him in return.

That was a treasure worth dying for. The ones from the lost city would be turned over to the authorities where they really belonged. And there would be more than enough money in it for Jean and himself—but that didn't matter.

He had all he wanted. All that he could ever want, in Jean.

"You know, darling," she murmured after another long kiss. "I'm going to like being called Jean Sheldon!"

"Not half as much as I'll like calling you that," he told her in a husky voice. He didn't say anything after that; there were more important matters to hold his attention.

Instead of any speeches, he took her up into his arms and carried her down the steps, along the corridor and into the captain's quarters.

Closing the door behind him, he moved over to the low bunk at the far wall.

"But I wanted to sunbathe some more," she objected, smiling and pulling him down to her.

"Believe me..." he softly whispered in her ear, "it'll get plenty hot in here after a while—"

She murmured contentedly and didn't say anything for a very long time.

ABOUT THE AUTHOR

Charles Nuetzel was born in San Francisco in 1934, and writes:

"As long as I can remember I wanted to be a writer. It was a dream I never thought would materialize. But with the help of Forrest J Ackerman, who became my agent, I managed to finally make it into print.

"I was lucky enough not only in selling my work to publishers but also ending up packaging books for some of them, and finally becoming a 'publisher' much like those who had bought my first novels. From there it as a simple leap to editing not only a science-fiction anthology, but also a line of SF books for Powell Sci-Fi back in the 1960s. Throughout these active professional years I had the chance to design some covers and do graphic cover layouts for pocket books & magazines."

Much of his work in covers and graphics are a result of having had a father who was a professional commercial artist, and who did a number of covers for sci-fi magazines in the 1950s and later for pocket books—even for some of Mr. Nuetzel's books.

In retirement he has become involved in swing dancing, a long time lover of Big Band jazz. But more interestingly world travels have taken him (and his wife Brigitte) across the world, to Hawaii, Caribbean, Mexico, Kenya, Egypt, Peru, having a lifelong interest in ancient civilizations. His website is full of thousands of pictures taken during these trips.

www.ingramcontent.com/pod-product-compliance
Lightning Source LLC
Chambersburg PA
CBHW051920240626
47153CB00004B/1297